Book One

EPIC ZERO

Tales of a Not-So-Super 6th Grader

By

R.L. Ullman

But That's
Another Story...
Press

Epic Zero: Tales of a Not-So-Super 6th Grader

Cover design by Yusup Mediyan
All character images created with heromachine.com.

Published by But That's Another Story... Press
Ridgefield, CT

Printed in the United States of America.

First Printing, 2015.

ISBN: 978-0-9964921-0-2
Library of Congress Control Number: 2015909607

For Matthew and Olivia,
never stop soaring

BOOKS BY R.L. ULLMAN

EPIC ZERO SERIES

Epic Zero: Tales of a Not-So-Super 6th Grader

Epic Zero Extra: Tales of a Superhero Screw Up
(exclusive novella at rlullman.com)

Epic Zero 2: Tales of a Pathetic Power Failure

Epic Zero 3: Tales of a Super Lame Last Hope

Epic Zero 4: Tales of a Total Waste of Time

Epic Zero 5: Tales of an Unlikely Kid Outlaw

MONSTER PROBLEMS SERIES

Monster Problems: Vampire Misfire

PRAISE FOR EPIC ZERO
Readers' Favorite Gold Medal Award Winner

"What a fun read! I knew this was a great children's/young adult book when my 11-year-old kept trying to read it over my shoulder. This is a delightful read for children and tweens, even for children who don't always enjoy reading. I loved the main character, I loved the message, I loved the illustrations; I just plain loved this book." **Rating: 5.0 stars by Tracy A. Fischer for Readers' Favorite.**

"An awesome and inspirational coming of age story filled with superheroes, arch villains and lots of action. Most highly recommended." **Rating: 5.0 stars by Jack Magnus for Readers' Favorite.**

"With Epic Zero, Ullman reminds me of why I used to love superheroes. If the other books are anything like this one, then the whole series will be great." **Rating 5.0 stars by Jessyca Garcia for Readers' Favorite.**

"As if a good read wasn't enough. Ullman goes that extra mile by adding illustrations and statistics, as well as a Meta glossary of terms and superpowers. These added features will appeal to those boys and girls who enjoy the science in science fiction." **Rating 5.0 stars by Francine Zane for Readers' Favorite.**

GET MORE EPIC!

Don't miss any of the Epic action!

Get a **FREE** copy of
Epic Zero Extra: Tales of a Superhero Screw Up,
only at rlullman.com.

TABLE OF CONTENTS

1.	I Hate My Birthday and Here's Why	1
2.	I Seem to Be Quite the Trouble Magnet	12
3.	I Do Something Astronomically Dumb	25
4.	I Put My New "Powers" on Speed Dial	37
5.	I Bite Off More Pain Than I Can Chew	46
6.	I Break the Law Into a Gazillion Pieces	57
7.	I Now Wish to Be Called Awesome Boy	68
8.	I Feel Like I Need to Die Now	79
9.	I Get the Shock of My Life	91
10.	I Lied, Now I Get the Shock of My Life	103
11.	I Attend an Alien Funeral	112
12.	I Go Straight to the Slammer	123
13.	I Battle a Slimy Worm to the Death	131
14.	I Take Control of Absolutely Everything	140
15.	I Doom the Entire Freaking Universe	152
Epilogue	Three Very Long Months Later…	163
Appendix	Meta Powers Glossary	170

ONE

I HATE MY BIRTHDAY AND HERE'S WHY

The alarm clock wails like a banshee, but I've been awake for hours. Without lifting my head from the pillow, I silence it with a well-practiced karate chop. I've stalled long enough. Just like on every other birthday I can remember, it's time to see if I've gained any Meta powers overnight. I take a deep breath. Then I launch into my standard testing routine.

I close my eyes tightly and then open them as wide as I can. No heat vision or pulsar beams come shooting out. *Not an energy manipulator.*

I flex my fingers and toes, but don't sense any mystical forces coursing through my veins. *Not magical.*

I try to remember last week's pre-algebra homework.

Can't remember—which is doubly depressing since I got a C the first time around. *Not super-intelligent.*

I carefully feel around my head, body and limbs. No evidence of sprouting horns, tail, or extra appendages. *Not a Meta-morph.*

I sit up, grab three tennis balls from a can next to my bed and start juggling. After keeping the balls in the air for a whopping three seconds, they all hit the ground and bounce limply away. No improvement to pre-existing poor hand-eye coordination. *Not a super-speedster.*

I stand up, walk over to my dresser and reach underneath. It's packed with clothes and probably weighs over 500 pounds. I count to three and lift with all my might. Dresser doesn't budge. Possibly broke my back. *Not super-strong.*

I jump on my bed, put my hands out like Superman and hurl myself across the room. I hit the floor hard, belly-flop style, knocking the wind out of me. Note to self, next year try the other way around—jump from floor onto bed. *Not a flyer.*

One more to go.

I close my eyes and concentrate on reading the mind of someone close by. I hear a loud knocking and then—

"Elliott Harkness, get out of bed you loser! You'll be late for school!" My sister, Grace, is at my door. No minds read. *Not a psychic.*

That makes me 0 for 8 on Meta powers. Another year, another epic failure.

I drag myself off the floor, pull on some clothes, and trudge into the bathroom. In the mirror, I find my unremarkable self staring right back at me—short and scrawny with a nest of brown hair and eyes the color of shoe leather. I look too young to be twelve, too plain to be popular and too ordinary to ever be a Meta.

You see, I live in a family of superheroes. We're part of a super team known as the Freedom Force, the greatest heroes ever assembled. In our lingo, a "Meta" stands for Meta-being, which is what we call a person, animal, or vegetable—don't laugh, it's happened—that possesses powers and abilities beyond what's considered normal. There are eight Meta types: Energy Manipulation, Flight, Magic, Meta-morphing, Psychic, Super-Intelligence, Super-Speed, and Super-Strength.

On top of that, there are three power levels: a Meta 1 has limited power, a Meta 2 has considerable power, and a Meta 3 has extreme power. If you don't have any powers at all, then you're known as a Meta 0. We call them "Zeroes" for short, which also stands for ordinary.

Just like me.

I turn out the lights and head for the Galley. I have fifteen minutes to scarf down some breakfast before school. When I get there, I find my super-family at their usual stations.

Mom is leaning against the fridge, arms crossed and brow furrowed, "packing" sandwiches into our lunch bags without using her hands. You see, Mom's a Meta 3 psychic who goes by the superhero handle Ms. Understood. Her powers include telekinesis, which allows her to move stuff around using only her mind, and also telepathy, so she can read other people's minds.

As you can imagine, having a mind-reading mom presents some serious challenges! She claims to use her powers only in the line of duty, but based on how often I seem to get in trouble, I suspect she isn't telling the whole truth on that one.

Like most mornings, she's already in full uniform, just waiting to see what evil the day brings. She wears a black bodysuit and mask to blend into the shadows, where she can put her deadly powers to work undetected. Plus, her superhero insignia looks like a giant eye, which not only intimidates the bad guys, but also makes you think twice about drinking milk straight from the carton!

Dad is ironing his cape by the breakfast nook. He takes law and order to a whole new level. On the law side, he's the leader of the Freedom Force and goes by the name Captain Justice. He's got Meta 3 super-strength with muscles so dense that he's pretty darn invulnerable. And, look out when the bullets start bouncing off of him!

On the order side, let's just say that he likes things tidy. His red, white and blue uniform must be crisply pressed, and there can be absolutely no dirt or smudges on his pristine, chest insignia of the golden scales of justice. He's so obsessive, he even lifts my furniture to hunt for dust bunnies! Like, someone please create a criminal distraction!

Grace, my fourteen-year-old sister, is perched on a stool, worshipping herself in a compact mirror. She's a Meta 2 flyer, but my parents expect her powers will eventually reach Meta 3 levels. She's still learning to be a hero, but lately seems much more interested in becoming an international celebrity. When she started out I suggested the name Self-Centered Lass, but she ignored me and chose Glory Girl. Glory Girl? Really? Please, get over yourself!

"Good morning, Elliott," Mom says.

"Morning," I say, waiting for some cursory acknowledgement that it's my special day. But there's nothing.

See, I know my life probably sounds glamorous and all, but trust me, it's not. Living with a bunch of do-gooders comes with some major drawbacks. At the top of the list is the fact that while superheroes are really great at the big things—like thwarting the forces of evil—they really stink at the little things.

Like, for example, remembering their kid's birthday.

I grab a cereal bar out of the pantry.

"Not hungry?" Mom asks.

"Nope," I say. "Not anymore."

"Well, Grace," Dad says. "Looks like you made the morning paper."

"I did?" Grace squeals with delight.

"You sure did," Dad says. "Look at this headline."

Grace snatches the paper and starts reading. "America's newest Meta-star does it again!' Wow! I look amazing!" She turns the paper to reveal the front page, featuring her in her Glory Girl outfit standing over an unconscious supervillain known as Catastro-flea. "Doesn't my costume totally pop?"

Truthfully, she did look kind of awesome in her crimson bodysuit featuring white shooting stars across her top and legs—her cape billowing perfectly in the wind. But, I wasn't ever going to tell her that.

"Looks like people are starting to take notice of your super-skills," Dad says.

"Maybe Captain Justice should hang up his tights," Mom jokes.

"You might be right, dear," Dad says. "Maybe I'll ride out my golden years in a Fortress of Solitude."

"Sure you will, Dad," Grace says, rolling her eyes. "I'll call Meta Meadows Retirement Home and see if they've got a spot for you. Hope you like tapioca."

"I haven't had tapioca since the Ghoulish Gourmet tried poisoning my dessert at the Mask of the Year Awards," Dad says. "On second thought, I've probably got a few more years of caped crusading in me."

"I figured you'd say that," Grace says. "Speaking of capes, I've been thinking about shaking up the whole hero thing. Maybe getting some brand sponsors and putting their logos on my costume. You know, like the sports stars do. Do you think I need an agent for that?"

"Grace, you know we don't work for money," Dad says.

"Oh, come on!" Grace says. "Aren't we allowed some perks with the job? I mean, we're on call, like, all the time."

Just then my phone vibrates in my pocket. It's a text message from TechnocRat:

<TechnocRat: Dog-Gone barfing in Mission Room. Can u clean up now?>

Dog-Gone is the name of our German Shepherd who has the power to turn invisible. One second he's sitting there, staring you down with his pitiful big-eyed begging act, the next he's gone. Conveniently, his powers seem to activate whenever food goes missing. I'm guessing he hijacked someone's breakfast when they weren't looking.

Cleaning up after Dog-Gone is bad enough, but doing it on my birthday just seems like cruel and unusual punishment. I should've gotten a super fish.

I exit the Galley to the West Wing stairwell, my sneakers echo down the fifty-five steps and five stair landings. Oh, I should probably mention that my house is kind of unusual. You see, we live in a satellite parked deep in outer space called the Waystation. The Waystation serves as the Freedom Force's headquarters, as well as the home away from home for most of the team.

You may be wondering why we're up here. Well, let's just say we do our jobs really well and there are plenty of creeps out there who'd love nothing more than to show up on our doorstep and try to settle the score. In fact, that's exactly what happened a few years back when the Slaughter Squad busted through the gates of our old headquarters on Earth. They almost had us, but that's why we moved to the Waystation—because up here we're *way* out of reach.

I stop at the utility closet to grab a mop, a bucket and some disinfectant because Dad's such a germaphobe. Knowing Dog-Gone, I'll probably have to wait around for all the invisible chunks to turn visible to be sure I don't miss anything. It takes me a while to collect the cleaning stuff because it's all shoved in the back, like someone wanted to hide it or something.

Finally, armed with everything I need to tackle the job, I make my way to the Mission Room and open the door.

"HAPPY BIRTHDAY!"

The cleaning supplies clang to the floor.

To my surprise, standing before me are all of the members of the Freedom Force: my parents, Grace, Shadow Hawk, TechnocRat, Blue Bolt, and Master Mime.

"Happy birthday, Elliott," Mom says.

"H-How?" I stammer.

"Tricked you, didn't I?" TechnocRat says, sitting on my dad's shoulder and stroking his whiskers with a smug look on his white, pointy, little face.

"What about Dog-Gone?" I ask.

"He's fine," Dad says. Dog-Gone appears from beneath the round conference table, his tail wagging a hundred miles per second. I swear he's smiling.

"You didn't think we'd forget your birthday, did you?" Mom asks.

I shrug. "Well..."

"Can we just get this over with?" Grace mutters.

"Grace, please," Dad says. "It's your brother's day."

Then, Master Mime uses his magic to conjure up a giant purple finger that flicks out the lights. Mom brings over a huge cake with twelve lit candles and everyone starts singing Happy Birthday, except for Master Mime and Dog-Gone, who obviously can't talk.

"Now make your wish," Mom says.

I close my eyes and take a deep breath when...

"Alert! Alert! Alert!" The alarm from the Meta Monitor blares through the Waystation. "Meta 2 disturbance. Power signature identified as Reptvillian. Alert! Alert! Alert!"

Before the lights even come back on, the Freedom Force springs into action. Blue Bolt and Master Mime are already gone. I just catch the flames from TechnocRat's jetpack and the silhouette of Shadow Hawk's cape as they disappear from the room. Dad and Grace leave without saying a word. I'm all alone with Mom who's still holding my cake.

"Elliott," she says. "I'm so sorry." Her eyes look sad, but her body's leaning towards the door. I can tell she wants to split.

"It's okay," I say. "Go ahead, somebody needs you."

She brushes my cheek. "My baby is so grown up."

I take the cake from her. "Oh," I say, "don't forget that Reptvillian is a Meta 2 on super-strength, but also a Meta 1 psychic, although he hasn't shown any evidence of telekinesis."

"Thanks for the tip," Mom says. "Don't be late for school." Then she winks and leaves.

I look down at the candles still burning on my cake. I never did make my wish. Not that it matters anyway.

I'm still a Zero.

FROM THE META MONITOR:

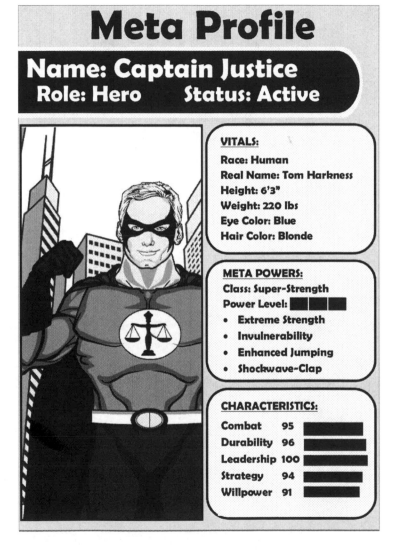

Meta Profile

Name: Captain Justice
Role: Hero   Status: Active

VITALS:

Race: Human
Real Name: Tom Harkness
Height: 6'3"
Weight: 220 lbs
Eye Color: Blue
Hair Color: Blonde

META POWERS:

Class: Super-Strength
Power Level: ▮▮▮
- Extreme Strength
- Invulnerability
- Enhanced Jumping
- Shockwave-Clap

CHARACTERISTICS:

Combat	95	
Durability	96	
Leadership	100	
Strategy	94	
Willpower	91	

TWO

I SEEM TO BE QUITE THE TROUBLE MAGNET

I can't decide what's worse, being abandoned on my birthday or watching Grace take off to save the day while I have to go to school. Yet, here I am, standing in the Transporter like a good little soldier, trying to make it to class before the attendance bell goes off. The Transporter is a teleportation system between the Waystation and Earth. It scans your body down to the subatomic level, scattering everything at point A and reassembling it at point B—all in a matter of seconds.

The Transporter, like the Waystation and every other gadget the Freedom Force uses, was designed by TechnocRat. It's amazing to think he was once just an ordinary rat in a secret government laboratory, but after being injected with an experimental brain tissue growth serum he became the smartest creature on the planet. He sometimes gets edgy with less intelligent people—also known as everyone else, and he hoards camembert cheese by the barrelful—the snobby, expensive kind, but the ideas that come out of his little noggin are astounding.

Moments later, I feel the pins-and-needles sensation of my atoms pushing back together. I watch the overhead console change from green to red and then the Transporter door slides open. Suddenly, I'm no longer in the Waystation at all, but am staring at the inside of a spacious suburban living room.

It has a large white sofa, two navy blue sitting chairs, a wooden coffee table and a flat screen TV. Against the far wall are bookcases filled with the classics and framed pictures of Grace and me as little kids. Every room in the house, from the kitchen to the bedrooms, is fully furnished. We even have spare clothes in the closets and shelf-stable food in the pantry... It's like we actually live here, but the beauty of it is, we don't. It's the Prop House.

We call it the Prop House because that's exactly what it is—a prop—designed to make people think it's our home. Our parents wanted us to attend regular school and try to be "normal." So, in order to be eligible for public school, we had to have a proper mailing address. That's where the Prop House comes in. No one knows it's just a front that houses the Transporter up to our real home on the Waystation.

To prevent anyone from discovering our true identities, my parents make routine appearances as suburbanites in the neighborhood; picking up the morning paper or mowing the lawn. On the rare occasion that someone rings the doorbell, deafening alarms blast through the Waystation. One of us—typically me being the only one around—then has to race to the Transporter and make it down to answer the Prop House door as if nothing's out of the ordinary. Usually, it's not a problem, but it can be awkward if you're in the middle of a shower, or worse, stuck on the can.

Note to self: I really need to talk to TechnocRat about installing an intercom system from the Waystation to the Prop House. Then I could talk to people and ask them to hang on a minute or, in the case of those annoying vacuum cleaner salesmen, just tell them to "get lost!"

I step into the living room and wrap my hand around a miniature Statue of Liberty model sitting on an end table. When I pull sideways the figurine makes a clicking noise and a gigantic mirror slides down from the ceiling, concealing the Transporter. Then I walk out the front door and lock it behind me.

It takes me five minutes to reach Keystone Middle School. It's week six of a forty week school year and I diligently check off each and every day on my wall calendar. The middle school pools three local elementary schools, which means there are three times the number of sixth-graders I try to avoid. Don't get me wrong, I can make friends if I want. But why bother? It's not like I can ever bring anyone back to my house to hang out.

Just then my phone buzzes. It's a text from Mom:

<Mom: Sorry about bday! Have a gr8 day! Luv u!>

It's not unusual for Mom to check up on me after a total parenting disaster like this morning. Believe me, I appreciate it, but I'm never quite sure if it's for my benefit or hers. I'm in the middle of texting her back when I run smack into what I think is a brick wall. Turns out it's another student.

"Sorry," I say.

"You got a problem?" rumbles a deep voice from high above.

"No," I answer, my neck craning so far back to see the kid's face I think my head's going to fall off. Angry eyes bear down from beneath a bushy unibrow that looks like it may flutter off and attack me. "I didn't mean to crash into your ... giganticness."

"You making fun of me?" says kid giant.

"Well, no, I ..."

Then I notice students circling around us. They're coming in waves, like sharks drawn to chum. I don't like where this is heading.

"You're annoying," kid giant says.

"You must be pen pals with my sister," I say. "Now how about we walk away and pretend this whole thing never happened?"

Then the kids start closing in, chanting "Fight! Fight! Fight!"

Great, now I'm the morning's entertainment. I want nothing more than to lift up into the air like Grace and fly out of here. But, of course, I can't. I'm a freaking Zero.

Kid giant grabs my shirt collar.

"Hey, c'mon!" I plead. "You don't want to do time for hurtin' little old me?"

Then I see his massive fist go back. And that's when everything goes dark.

***

Well, I may be the first kid in history to be hospitalized for fainting during a fight. The nurse told me I apparently crumpled to the ground right before the big lug swung at me and was rescued by the Cafeteria Lady who happened to be in the parking lot pushing a cart of strawberry milk.

It's just so embarrassing on so many levels.

And to top it off, my mom had to leave the Freedom Force to meet me at the hospital while they ensured I didn't have a concussion. After taking me home to the Waystation and confining me to bed rest, she left me alone with my neurotic thoughts. Now all I can do is sit and wonder what creative nicknames my classmates are going to bestow upon me tomorrow.

Elliott the Unconscious? Harkness the Horizontal? The Narcoleptic Kid? The possibilities seem endless.

And, oh, the fun Grace is going to have with this one.

After several hours of reliving my nightmare over and over again against the backdrop of mindless cartoons, I'm antsy to get out of here. I need to do something to take my mind off it all and I know just the thing!

I yank off the covers when Dog-Gone, who's curled up at my feet, gives a low growl.

"Oh, knock it off," I say. "I don't care what Mom told you. I'm getting out of bed."

Dog-Gone turns invisible. The dude who said dogs are man's best friend clearly never met mine.

"Hang on," I say. "I'll give you a treat if you don't tell her."

Dog-Gone reappears with a cocked ear. But then he disappears again. That dog really knows how to work a bribe.

"Two treats," I say quickly. But he doesn't show. Not that I expect him to anyway because I know what he's really after. "I'm not giving you the whole bag," I say. "You'll get sick. Three treats or nothing and that's my final offer."

After a few seconds, the mercenary reappears, his tail wagging in victory.

"Okay, then. Follow me. And be quiet about it."

Trust me, sneaking around when there's a Meta 3 psychic on the premises is no easy task. I can only hope Mom is caught up in some complicated forensics analysis or something and won't bother mind-linking with me.

We make it safely down to the Galley where I pay off my debt of three doggie treats. I tell Dog-Gone to make himself invisible, and then I tip-toe my way up to the Monitor Room. This will definitely take my mind off of things.

You see, the Monitor Room houses the Meta Monitor, which is our one-of-a-kind computer system that operates like a burglar alarm on steroids for detecting super powers. The Meta Monitor constantly searches for disturbances in the Earth's molecular structure. Like the uniqueness of fingerprints, each and every super power leaves a distinct and detailed signature. The Meta Monitor reads this signature and then matches it with its extensive database of Metas to determine who, or what, may have caused it.

Currently, there are four hundred and thirty-two villains in the database. Two hundred and seventy-one are under lock and key. Ninety-nine are considered inactive—in other words, they either got out of the game, were wheeled off to an old age home, or vanished off the face of the Earth. That leaves sixty-two bona fide nut jobs out there who are completely unaccounted for and just waiting to stir up trouble.

How do I know all this? Well, I guess you can call Meta-mining my hobby. I've spent countless hours digging through the database, studying up on every villain I could; memorizing their origins, aliases, powers, weaknesses, fighting tendencies and so on. I figure if I'm going into the family business, then I should probably have this stuff down cold. Plus, it beats the pants off of doing homework.

The Meta Monitor has state-of-the-art telescopes that can pick up visuals of any point on the Earth's surface. I key in a few commands and the screen begins rotating through a number of famous landmarks. The White House; The U.S. Capitol; The Hoover Dam; Mount Rushmore. Everything looks peachy. Nothing suspicious. Maybe if I fish where the fish are?

I punch in some more commands and up pops an image of a gigantic prison. It's known as Lockdown, or more formally, Lockdown Meta-Maximum Federal Penitentiary. It's the only super-maximum-security prison specifically designed to contain the world's most dangerous Metas. Dad told me that Lockdown almost didn't happen. The skeptics didn't believe that one place could safely hold so many super-powered criminals. After all, the potential for something to go horribly wrong increases dramatically when only a few feet of concrete separate the most evil beings on the planet.

Over time, however, Lockdown has more than proven its worth. One reason for this is TechnocRat, who designs each and every cell to neutralize the special abilities of its occupant. For example, if a villain has Meta 3 super strength, then his or her cell is outfitted with super-malleable walls designed to absorb the energy of a power punch and send it back with twice the force.

Two

TechnocRat can devise a way to contain any criminal. And fortunately, its worked every time.

The other reason is my dad. His day job as warden of Lockdown allows him to keep close tabs on the inmates. Of course, his Meta identity is a secret so none of the villains know that he's the one who put them there in the first place.

It's also a well-guarded secret that the only set of blueprints for Lockdown and the way out of each and every cell is stored in a special vault right here on the Waystation. That's another reason our headquarters is in space. It keeps the prisoners on Earth and their escape plans in orbit.

Well, it seems like there's nothing doing at the prison either. Perhaps—

"Elliott Harkness!"

I jump a foot off my chair.

Busted.

I turn around to find Mom standing with her hands on her hips, also known as full anger pose. Dog-Gone is by her side. I should've given that mutt four treats.

"Just what do you think you're doing?" Mom asks. "You're supposed to be in bed."

"I'm bored," I answer.

"And since when does boredom give you permission to ignore the doctor's orders?" she asks.

"Um, when I'm really bored?" I answer. "Besides, I thought you might have sent a telepathic hint to my mind

suggesting it would be okay. So, whose fault is this really?" I smile. She doesn't. Never, *ever*, try reverse psychology on a psychic.

"Okay, okay." I set the Meta Monitor on auto-pilot and slide off the chair. "Nothing ever happens on my watch any—"

"Alert! Alert! Alert!" the Meta Monitor blares. "Meta 3 disturbance. Repeat: Meta 3 disturbance. Power signature identified as Meta-Taker. Alert! Alert! Alert! Meta 3 disturbance. Power signature identified as Meta-Taker."

"Really?" I say. "Like that couldn't have happened a minute ago?"

"Elliott, not now," Mom says, racing to the console. It looks like she's seen a ghost.

She hits a few buttons and a visual of the villain called Meta-Taker appears. The first thing I notice is the outfit. He's wearing a dark hooded cloak, like some sort of monk. But when he moves, you can see massive muscles rippling beneath his robes. Then, the camera pulls in closer and I do a double take.

His skin and hair are pale white, like bone—and a strange orange energy that seems to have a life of its own blazes around his eyes. For his tremendous size he's surprisingly graceful, yet there's something robotic about him. And he's standing near a gigantic hole in the ground which makes the whole scene look like the Grim Reaper surfacing from the underworld itself.

Dog-Gone growls.

"Um, Mom. What's up with that guy?"

"His name is Meta-Taker," she practically whispers. "He's the most powerful enemy we've ever faced. We thought he was dead ... buried alive ... it's been over twenty years."

"Well, I can assure you, he ain't dead," I offer.

"No, he's not," she says, her voice quickening. "I'm activating the distress signal."

As soon as she says that, I know it's serious. Each member of the Freedom Force wears a special nano-communicator housed inside an everyday object—like a watch or a necklace—which produces vibrational patterns signaling different things. The distress signal is reserved for the most urgent of issues and directs the team to head immediately to the Waystation—do not pass go—do not collect 200 dollars.

"I need to get ready," Mom says.

"I'll help," I say.

"No," she says forcefully. "This isn't a game. This is a job for the Freedom Force."

I look down. The words sting.

"Elliott," she says, grabbing my hands. "Trust me. You need to stay here, where it's safe, and rest up. Keep an eye on Dog-Gone."

"I understand," I say reluctantly. "Be careful."

"I will," she answers, squeezing my hands before leaving.

I take a deep breath. Dog-Gone and I stare at the

image of Meta-Taker.

I heard what she said, but I'm getting awfully tired of sitting on the sidelines.

Then a light bulb goes off.

"You know what, old boy," I say. "You're not the only one here that's good at hiding."

Meta Profile

Name: Ms. Understood
Role: Hero   Status: Active

VITALS:

Race: Human
Real Name: Kate Harkness
Height: 5'6"
Weight: 130 lbs
Eye Color: Brown
Hair Color: Brown

META POWERS:

Class: Psychic
Power Level: ■ ■ ■

- Extreme Telepathy
- Extreme Telekinesis
- Group Mind-Linking
- Long-Range Capability

CHARACTERISTICS:

Combat	80	
Durability	42	
Leadership	88	
Strategy	85	
Willpower	95	

THREE

I DO SOMETHING ASTRONOMICALLY DUMB

While the team assembles for a briefing in the Mission Room, I buy Dog-Gone's silence—this time with five doggie treats—and stow away on the Freedom Flyer. The Freedom Flyer is the rocket-powered shuttle we sometimes use to get from the Waystation to Earth and back again. It's spacious enough to hold the entire team and is outfitted with weapons and reflector shields in case of attack. It can also really motor, reaching the upper limits of supersonic speed at Mach 5.0.

This shuttle is actually Freedom Flyer II. Freedom Flyer I is grounded in the Hangar due to some steering column damage that happened when Master Mime used it as a battering ram against the Brutal Birdmen. After that episode, TechnocRat revoked Master Mime's pilot's license.

The Freedom Flyer II is designed to be more durable than the original, but more importantly, it has a larger supply compartment big enough to fit yours truly.

Now I just have to wait for the team to show up.

Since I've got the time, I download Meta-Taker's profile to my mobile. I realized that I'd never come across his record before because it wasn't logged in the active database at all, but instead was in the file of deceased Metas. After a few seconds the profile appears. It reads:

- *Name: Meta-Taker*
- *Real Name: Unknown*
- *Height: 8'0"*
- *Weight: 1,200 lbs*
- *Eye Color: Orange*
- *Hair Color: White*
- *Meta Class: Meta-morph*
- *Known Powers: Can duplicate the power of any Meta in his immediate vicinity. Can duplicate the powers of multiple Metas at once which may result in a cumulative power build if Metas are of a similar power type. This may result in Meta 4 power levels.*

I stop and read that section again:

This may result in Meta 4 power levels.

What??

I've never even heard of Meta 4. I didn't even know it was possible. If Meta 3 is classified as extreme power then what is Meta 4? God-like? No wonder Mom turned as white as a ghost. I keep reading:

• *Known Weaknesses: None*

• *Origin: Unknown*

• *Background: A being of unparalleled power, Meta-Taker emerged with the sole purpose of ruling Earth by eliminating its Meta hero population. With powers too strong for any one hero to stop, a group of heroes banded together with the united goal of ending his rampage. They called themselves the Freedom Force. Despite heavy casualties, the Freedom Force eventually subdued the villain, burying him alive thousands of feet below the Earth's surface.*

• *Known Crimes: Responsible for the murders of original Freedom Force members Dynamo Joe, Madame Meteorite, Robot X-treme, Rolling Thunder and Sunbolt.*

• *Status: Assumed deceased*

I swallow hard. It dawns on me that I've never asked my parents how the Freedom Force came together in the first place. Ever since I can remember they've always been there. They're the good guys. The idea that heroes can die never even crossed my mind.

Right now, hanging with Dog-Gone is beginning to sound better and better. I decide to split, but when I move to pop open the compartment door, the team boards the Freedom Flyer.

I'm trapped!

Just. Freaking. Wonderful.

If Mom finds me, I'm dead meat. And, Grace will have an absolute field day at my expense. Better to stay quiet and sneak out once the mission is over and we're back safe and sound at the Waystation. Just then, I hear the hatch close so I brace myself for take-off.

My thoughts wander back to Meta-Taker. If he was buried thousands of feet below ground then how did he get out? Had he been clawing his way to the surface for the last twenty years? Didn't he need to eat and breathe?

Before I can figure it out, we've landed. I hear muffled voices from the team, including Grace's over-confident platitudes, and then the hatch opens. I get bounced around as they file out of the Freedom Flyer.

After a few minutes, I open the compartment door and confirm the cockpit is empty. I move to the front and duck behind the pilot's chair so I can safely look out the front windshield without being seen.

We've touched down at some sort of construction site. To the side, I can see the hole Meta-Taker emerged from. It looks much bigger in person, like it was made by some kind of giant mole or something. But as fascinating as that is, I'm here for the main event, which is unfolding about a hundred yards away.

The Freedom Force is circled around Meta-Taker, giving him a wide berth. Meta-Taker stands calmly in the center, that freakish orange energy crackling wildly from his eyes. But even more freakishly, despite the threat of all the heroes around him, his face is expressionless.

Dad is calling out. He's ordering Meta-Taker to surrender, but the brute isn't responding. Dad picks up a nearby pick-up truck and throws it at Meta-Taker, who reaches out casually and catches it like a Frisbee. Then he tears it in half like paper.

That's when the other heroes jump in.

Nearly faster than my eye can track, Blue Bolt launches at Meta-Taker. She's the fastest Meta alive and wears a lightning bolt on her costume because she strikes at super-charged speed. I once clocked her circling the globe in ten seconds flat, which is ten times longer than it takes her to eat a double cheeseburger.

Meta-Taker, however, isn't impressed. He duplicates Blue Bolt's power and swings at her like he's playing baseball without a bat. There's a massive popping sound and then all I see is a blue streak flying through the sky. It looks like she'll land hundreds of miles away.

Then Master Mime steps into the fray. His parents died when he was a teenager, and he took up street miming to survive. One day, he found a strange purple amulet in his tip jar. With the amulet, Master Mime discovered he could conjure hard-light energy constructs in any form he could imagine. And with all his years of miming, he's a must-have partner on the Waystation for charades.

I watch Master Mime forge a javelin of purple energy

and hurl it at Meta-Taker. But the villain has already duplicated Master Mime's powers, forming a shield of purple energy that easily blocks the javelin, shattering it in half. Then Meta-Taker creates an energy lasso and hog-ties Master Mime, sending him crashing into Shadow Hawk.

With those heroes out of the way, Meta-Taker uses Master Mime's powers to make a massive energy hammer and tries to pound the remaining good guys. My parents and TechnocRat dive for cover, barely avoiding being flattened. This isn't going well.

And then I realize, I haven't seen Grace.

She wasn't standing in the original circle and isn't in the fight. I look high above, but can't spot her in the air. My heart starts beating fast. Where is she? Is she hurt? Or dead? I need to find her!

I punch the hatch release, jump out of the shuttle, and land on top of something I'm not expecting to be there. The impact of my hand hitting skull dislodges my phone from my grasp. I tumble onto my backside.

Sitting up, I'm suddenly staring at a short, bug-eyed, bald man with crooked teeth and a more crooked nose. He's wearing a reddish-brown costume covered in some kind of goopy slime. Although I've never seen him before, he seems oddly familiar. Then my mind clicks to his Meta profile.

It's the Worm.

The Worm is a small-time criminal, a Meta 1 meta-morph with the unusual ability to secrete mucous from his pores, allowing him to tunnel through the ground like an earthworm. He's mostly wanted for street muggings and the occasional bank job. What's he doing here?

Then I realize there's something even stranger hanging around his neck. At first it looks like a Christmas ornament on a chain, but then I realize it's some sort of orb. It's smooth and white and pulsating. My eyes are drawn to it. I can't turn away. It's absolutely mesmerizing.

"Who are you?" the Worm says, snapping me back to reality.

"Stay away!" I yell, scrambling to my feet.

"You scared of me?" the Worm says, flashing an ear-to-ear grin.

"Back off!" I shout, looking for somewhere to run. "I'm a Meta!"

"A Meta, huh?" says the Worm, clutching the orb. "You look like a lost little boy to me." Then he lurches forward. "Boo!"

I take off.

I'm not looking where I'm going. I'm just trying to get as much distance between me and the Worm as possible. And that's when I feel a meaty hand grab me by the back of the collar and lift me high into the air.

The next thing I know, I'm gazing into the wild eyes of Meta-Taker.

"Let me go!" I scream, trying to kick free.

But Meta-Taker doesn't respond. He just stares at me,

and I'm helpless to do anything but stare right back. To my horror, he's even more frightening up close. His teeth are like knives, each one sharpened to a skin-piercing point. His breath is foul, like he's swallowed a barge of rotten fish. And his eyes—his eyes are like doorways to the gates of Hell.

"Elliott!" I can hear Mom's surprised scream.

"Release him!" Dad commands.

But Meta-Taker isn't interested in what he has to say.

"Please," I plead. "Let me go. I don't have powers. I'm just a Zero."

I look over at my parents. They're frozen.

"Drop the boy and take me," Dad says, inching closer with his hands in the air. "He has nothing for you, Meta-Taker."

Meta-Taker's eyes narrow. It's as if he's sensing me—studying me. Then his orange flames crackle slowly towards me. I push hard against his massive body, but I can't break free. The flames dance across my skin and then seep inside my mouth. I feel a warm sensation flush through me. My body feels paralyzed!

But, suddenly, the brute stops cold and looks at me strangely.

And then his flames snuff out.

Meta-Taker registers a look of surprise. And then, he clutches his head and screams in agony, dropping me hard to the ground.

"I'm inside!" Mom shouts. "I don't know how, but

I'm in! Now! Do it now!"

"Glory Girl!" Dad calls into the open air.

Right then, out of nowhere, a crimson streak falls from the sky and catches Meta-Taker off-guard, pushing him back towards the very hole he came out of. Meta-Taker teeters at the edge, and then stumbles over backwards, disappearing into the abyss.

"Quick," Dad says. "Bury him!"

The heroes combine their powers to fill in the hole with as much dirt and debris as they can find. The immediate threat is neutralized.

"TechnocRat," Dad says. "We need a cell to contain him. And fast."

"Working on it, Captain," says the little rat, flipping open a computer mounted on his jetpack.

"Great job, Glory Girl," Dad says. "Holding you in reserve kept your powers hidden from Meta-Taker and added the element of surprise we needed."

Grace beams. She's the hero.

And I'm the goat.

Mom runs over to me. "Elliott, are you okay? What in the world are you doing here?"

"I don't know, Mom," I answer. "I really don't know."

Just then, a large fly buzzes around my head a few times and drops on my knee. It stares at me with its big, green eyes before I shoo it away. Strangely, it doesn't leave. It hovers for a few seconds, probably feeling sorry for me, and then it looks at me, looks at my mom, looks at me again, and takes off.

It's been that kind of a day.

Mom kneels down and hugs me. "Thank goodness, you're okay."

"Elliott, you're grounded," Dad says. "That was irresponsible. You could have gotten yourself or someone else killed."

"That's fine," I mutter, accepting my punishment. I deserve whatever book they're going to throw at me.

"I don't know what happened," Mom says with a shudder. "I couldn't get inside his head for the longest time, and then all of the sudden, I could. The anger inside of him was so intense."

Then I remember the Worm and that weird orb.

"Hey," I say. "You wouldn't believe who else was here. The Worm! We've got to catch him!"

"The Worm?" Dad says, looking around. "That lowlife? He must have been passing through. This fight was way out of his league. I'm guessing he slithered away happy not be mixed up in all of this."

For some reason I wasn't so sure, but after all the trouble I'd caused I decide to keep my mouth shut.

"Why don't the three of you head back to the Waystation," Dad says. "We'll find Blue Bolt and wrap it up from here."

Mom, Grace and I head up the Freedom Flyer ramp. Right before we take off I remember I had dropped something. My phone!

I lower the hatch and, after a few minutes of frantic searching, find it tucked beneath a rock. It looks a little more beaten up then I remember, but then again, so am I.

FROM THE META MONITOR:

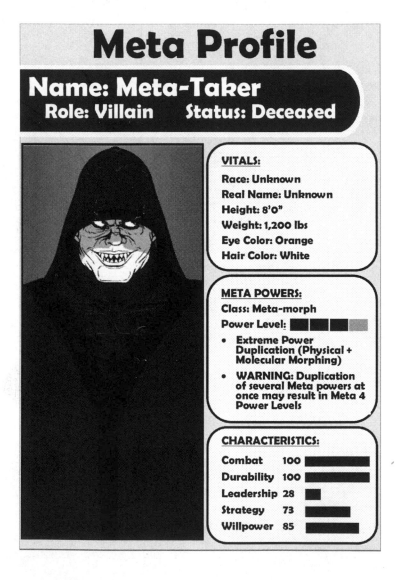

Meta Profile

Name: Meta-Taker
Role: Villain   Status: Deceased

VITALS:

Race: Unknown
Real Name: Unknown
Height: 8'0"
Weight: 1,200 lbs
Eye Color: Orange
Hair Color: White

META POWERS:

Class: Meta-morph
Power Level: ■ ■ ■ □

- **Extreme Power Duplication (Physical + Molecular Morphing)**
- **WARNING: Duplication of several Meta powers at once may result in Meta 4 Power Levels**

CHARACTERISTICS:

Combat	100	
Durability	100	
Leadership	28	
Strategy	73	
Willpower	85	

FOUR

I PUT MY NEW "POWERS" ON SPEED DIAL

After tossing and turning, hopelessly trying to erase the day's events from my mind, I finally manage to doze off only to be woken moments later by my phone that's vibrating on the nightstand like a rabid woodpecker. Half asleep, I lift my head, fresh drool running down my chin, wondering what all the ruckus is about. Only the Freedom Force has my number and they returned hours ago after depositing Meta-Taker in his cozy new prison accommodations at Lockdown.

So, I'm clueless about who's texting me.

Clawing for my mobile, I palm it and pull it close. The light from the display panel temporarily blinds me, but my eyes adjust quickly to find ten text messages and more coming in by the second:

>Taser: Big score 2nite. Anyone in? ☺<

>Brawler: Pizza? Where? Time?<

>Taser: No idiot! Bank job. Keystone Savings. 11PM.<

>Makeshift: Tx for invite. What about Freedom Force?<

>Brawler: U not bringing pizza? ☹ <

>Taser: Not concerned about FF. Small job.<

>Taser: And no pizza!!!<

>Makeshift: What's the split?<

>Taser: 33% each.<

>Makeshift: I want 60%. U clearly need help.<

>Taser: 40% max.<

>Makeshift: 55%.<

>Brawler: How about doughnuts?<

>Taser: 45%.<

>Makeshift: Forget it. Need 2 wash parrot 2nite.<

>Taser: Fine. 50%?<

>Makeshift: See u at 11! ☺<

At first, I have no clue what's happening. And then it hits me like a ton of bricks. This isn't my phone. It's the Worm's! They must have been the same color and the same brand. We must have mixed them up when we collided!

The only sound I hear is my heart thumping against my chest. I throw off the covers, jump out of bed and start pacing. As if this whole mess couldn't possibly get any worse, Mom and Dad are literally going to kill me if they find out a villain has my phone! They'll have me drawn and quartered, and then they'll take my quarters and draw and quarter them again.

Another text comes across. I tap the button to read it when I realize something's wrong. Where's the security code screen? There's no security code screen?

Wait, there's no security code screen! My phone has a security code screen! And then I remember I'd set it to wipe the device after three failed security code attempts.

Yes! Yes! Yes! I may get to live!

I flop down on the bed, relief washing over me. But I still need to tell my parents. They have a right to know that an official piece of Freedom Force property has fallen into the hands of a known criminal. That would be the right thing to do. But then again ...

The Worm isn't really a threat, is he? I mean, c'mon, it's the Worm. A Meta 1. I'm sure he messed up the security code by now and erased all the data. So do I really need to tell my parents? I can just say my phone got obliterated in the battle by some rogue laser beam and now I need a new one. Then they can still get in touch with me, and I can hold on to this one! I look down at The Worm's phone. More texts:

>Brawler: Never heard back on the doughnuts?<
>Taser: NO DOUGHNUTS U IDIOT!!!!!!!!!<
>Brawler: Ok. U don't have 2 yell! ☹<

I stay up all night flipping through the Worm's contact list and trolling through his texts. Most of it's in shorthand, but I manage to identify his ordinary contacts like his mom, his dry cleaner, his favorite Mexican restaurant, his barber—don't know why a bald man needs a barber—from his Meta contacts.

By the end of it, I'm pretty sure that Taser is the Meta 1 energy manipulator that can shoot electric currents from his hands. And, Brawler is the Meta 1 strongman that gets his strength from radioactive beer. But I can't find any reference to whoever "Makeshift" is. However, it's clear from their group texts that they've been talking about pulling off a job for a while, but have never gotten it together. They also use a lot of freaking profanity.

But despite all of my searching, I'm not able to find anything linking the Worm to Meta-Taker. Maybe Dad's right. Maybe the Worm was just in the wrong place at the wrong time. But there's something strange about that orb. What is it and what's the Worm doing with it? I can't shake the feeling that there's something more to this story.

Something I'm missing.

At this point, I'm completely bleary-eyed when my alarm goes off. Somehow, morning snuck up on me which means it's time to get ready for school. Oh. Joy. I wait a few minutes and my second alarm comes right on schedule.

There's a knock at my door.

"Hey, *Powerless Boy*," Grace says mockingly. "Get up or you're gonna be late!"

I look down at the Worm's phone.

Powerless Boy, huh? Maybe. But then again, maybe not …

I dress quickly and head down to the Galley for breakfast. After my screw-up the day before, I know this isn't going to be pleasant.

"Good morning, Elliott," Mom says. "How are you feeling?"

"Um, kind of tired," I answer. "And sore."

"Remember, Elliott," Dad says sternly. "You're grounded. I expect you home right after school."

"I know," I say. Truthfully, being grounded didn't mean much. I'm always home right after school anyway.

"And no monitor duty," he adds.

"Got it," I say. Well, that part sucks.

"Look for me on the five o'clock news," Grace says smugly. "They want to interview me about how I saved the world from Meta-Taker."

"Oh, I'll be sure to tune in for that," I say with dripping sarcasm as I grab a cereal bar and stuff it into my backpack. I sit down at the table and take a deep breath. Here goes nothing. "Oh, I almost forgot. I need a new phone. Mine was vaporized by one of Master Mime's energy sprockets."

"Okay, just get one from TechnocRat," Dad says.

"Cool." Whew! That was easy. Now for part two. "I also had the weirdest dream last night."

"Really," says Dad, not lowering his paper. "What kind of dream?"

"Well," I say. "I had this dream that Keystone Savings Bank was going to get robbed. I had this really clear image that three Metas were involved."

Dad lowers his paper a little. "That *is* weird."

"Yeah," I say. "There were three guys. All Meta 1's. An energy manipulator, a really strong brutish guy, and one I couldn't make out too clearly, but seemed kind of harmless."

Dad and Mom look at each other.

"I feel like it might happen tonight. Around eleven."

"At eleven?" Mom says with a surprised look. "Well, that's certainly specific. Okay. I guess we'll keep our eyes and ears open."

There, the seed is planted.

"Hogwash!" Grace says. "Your brain must've bounced when Meta-Taker dropped you on it." She scoops up her backpack and races for the Transporter. "Later peeps, I've gotta split!"

I grab my bag and chase her down, managing to make it right before the door shuts. We travel in silence and re-atomize at the Prop House.

"Are you such a loser that you have to make up stories for attention?" Grace says. "It must really suck being you."

She walks outside and looks both ways to make sure no one's around, and then takes off into the air, leaving me alone on the front stoop. I lock the door and head off to school.

All of a sudden, my phone starts going nuts again. More texts:

>Taser: Anyone got smoke bomb?<

>Makeshift: Nope.<

>Brawler: Yes. Why?<

>Taser: Need for job.<

>Brawler: 4 2nite?<

>Taser: No 4 gopher in my garden. YES 2NITE!!!!<

>Brawler: Still yelling! ☹<

That actually makes me chuckle.

Then my cell is yanked right out of my hands.

"Well, look who came back," kid giant says, tossing my phone from one over-sized mitt to the other. "It's the wimpy kid. I got a week's detention because of you. And the Cafeteria Lady's been giving me the stink eye."

I stay calm despite my inner sense of panic. I need that phone back! Without it, I can't keep pretending I have powers. "Listen," I say. "I'm sure I can avoid injury and you can avoid incarceration if you simply give me the phone and we go our separate ways."

Another crowd starts forming. Here we go again.

"Uh-uh," he says, dangling the phone in front of me, "If you want it, come and get it."

I reach out and he steps backwards. The other kids laugh. He holds it out and I try again. Same result. He's baiting me. Toying with me.

"C'mon," I say. "We're going to be late for class."

"This is much more fun than class," he snorts.

Just then, a girl I've never seen before strides forward. She's a little taller than me and is dressed kind of preppy with a white oxford shirt and slim, dark-washed jeans. She's really pretty, with long dark hair falling in ringlets to her shoulders. I have no idea what she's doing.

She looks at me with her bright, green eyes and says, "You heard him. If you want your phone, take it from him."

But I don't move. I'm so shocked she's talking to me that I'm glued to the spot.

Suddenly, the girl steps forward, punches kid giant in the gut and says, "If you tell on me, I'll do it again. But harder next time."

Kid giant topples over, struggling to catch his breath.

"Never show weakness," she says. And then she hands me my phone and walks away.

FROM THE META MONITOR:

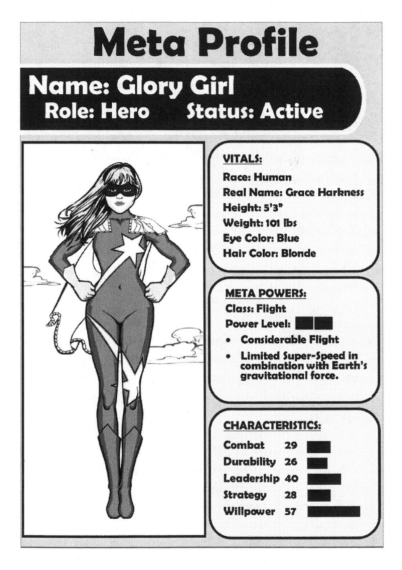

Meta Profile

Name: Glory Girl
Role: Hero   Status: Active

VITALS:

Race: Human
Real Name: Grace Harkness
Height: 5'3"
Weight: 101 lbs
Eye Color: Blue
Hair Color: Blonde

META POWERS:

Class: Flight
Power Level: ■ ■
- **Considerable Flight**
- **Limited Super-Speed in combination with Earth's gravitational force.**

CHARACTERISTICS:

Combat	29	■
Durability	26	■
Leadership	40	■
Strategy	28	■
Willpower	57	■

FIVE

I BITE OFF MORE PAIN THAN I CAN CHEW

The texts keep rolling in all day. There are threads about bank vault designs, security camera locations, getaway routes and contingency plans should a good guy show up. Everything finally settles down at four o'clock. Their plan is set.

And I'm home alone. Grounded.

Well, I guess Dog-Gone is around, but he disappeared after eating my cereal when I went to the bathroom. The school day was a total blur. Aside from keeping up with the flurry of text messages, I found myself thinking a lot about that girl from this morning.

She ended up being in my Social Studies class. That's where I learned her name was Cammie and she'd just moved to town. She seems really smart and raised her hand a lot to answer questions. She didn't look my way once.

I keep thinking about what she said. *Never show weakness.* Does she think I'm weak? Deep down, I know the answer. I never stand up for myself. Not to Grace. Not to that bully. Not to anyone. Maybe it's time I started.

Being grounded was infinitely more boring than just being home on a regular day, and I was getting tired of sitting around twiddling my thumbs. Dad said I can't do monitor duty, but he didn't say anything about the Combat Room.

The Combat Room is on the lowest level of the Waystation. It's where the Freedom Force hones their powers and practices their fighting skills. The Combat Room was designed by TechnocRat and uses advanced holographic technology reinforced with force fields to project hard images that look and feel real. The Combat Room can create any situation imaginable, from a run-of-the-mill street mugging to an all-out Meta villain assault. While I've watched countless hours of Combat Room training from the safety of playback video, I was never allowed to participate in an actual combat scenario.

Today that's about to change.

I enter the Combat Room and take a deep breath. The room is massive, equivalent to a large aircraft hangar. The entire space is stark white with no windows or doors—

Five

except for the one I came in from. It's also eerily silent.

Until you make GISMO aware of your presence.

"GISMO," I call, my voice echoing through the vast chamber.

There's a low hum followed by a series of beeps.

"GISMO online," came a warm, mechanical voice. "Good afternoon, Elliott Harkness."

GISMO is short for Global Intelligence Simulation Model Operator. GISMO was designed to run the Combat Room. It's GISMO's job to track the progress of participants through the simulation. If things are going well, GISMO can make the challenge more difficult. If things are going poorly, GISMO can end the simulation with a simple voice command.

Now all I need to do is pick a training module. The words "never show weakness" stick in my mind.

"GISMO," I say. "Please load training module SS12."

There's a pause.

"Simulation warning," GISMO states. "Training module SS12 is an intermediate module for Meta's possessing super strength."

"Yes, GISMO," I answer. "I understand. Please load training module SS12."

Another pause.

"GISMO is not authorized to load training module SS12 for Elliott Harkness. Elliott Harkness does not possess Meta level super str—"

"Override sequence B321ZFINAL," I command.

"Module loading," GISMO replies.

You pick up all sorts of tricks hanging out with TechnocRat.

The barren room instantly transforms into a dark, smoky saloon filled with large, tough-looking men covered in tattoos. Some are drinking beer while others are playing pool. One of them is even wearing an eye-patch. I'm lost in the power of the simulation. The flickering neon lights. The music blaring in the background. The smack of pool balls colliding.

I check out the bar and notice all the seats are taken except for one way down at the end where a strange woman is standing. Her face seems young, but her hair is long and silver. She's dressed in a dark business suit with white, vertical pinstripes. She looks totally out of place, which probably means that she's somehow important to this simulation module. So, I mosey on down and take the seat beside her.

"What'll it be, buddy?" asks the bartender, a beefy man missing several important teeth.

I've never ordered a drink from a bar before. I look over at the woman. She's watching so I can't blow it.

"I'll have a Shirley Temple, please," I say. "Shaken, not stirred."

"Right," says the Bartender, rolling his eyes.

"Hang on," I say, turning to my companion. "Let me see what the lady would like."

"Oh, I am no drinker like you," she says with a strange accent. It sounds almost like Russian, but I'm not really sure.

I nod and the bartender goes to fix my beverage.

After a few seconds, the woman speaks. "Tell me. Are you the one?"

"What one?" I ask. I don't know what she's talking about.

The bartender brings my drink. I take a sip.

"Do not be funny, boy," she says. "Are you the one sent by the Emperor? Are you the Meta who will help me find the orb?"

I do a spit take.

Did she just say *orb*?

"I knew it," she says angrily. "I knew it as soon as I saw you. You are too puny. Too small."

"Now hang on, Lady," I say. "I'm a member of the Freedom Force."

"I knew the Emperor would betray me," she continues. "He will pay eventually. But you must pay now. Comrades, kill him!"

Well, that doesn't sound good. All of a sudden, I have a flashback of Dad warning me to stay out of the Combat Room because it's possible to be knocked out, or even killed, during the simulation!

I leap off my chair just as all the goons in the bar surround me. My heart is pounding so hard I think it's going to burst out of my chest and fly straight out of the saloon. There's no time to think. The man with the eye patch is standing in front of me, waving a pool cue over my head.

Then, he swings at me.

I duck and the cue shatters against the bar. A piece ricochets and hits me hard in the jaw. That hurt! This is for real! This guy's actually trying to kill me!

"Get him, fools!" the woman commands.

Another guy lunges at me, but I somersault between his legs and kick him from behind, sending him headfirst into a chair. "Take that!" I yell, sort of impressed with myself. But, there's no time to pat myself on the back. I'm well outnumbered. I look for an opening, but there's none to be found.

"You are no Meta," the woman says. "You are just a boy. Soon to be a very *dead* boy."

I have to get out of here. But how? And then I notice the eye-patched man. If I can charge his blind side then maybe, just maybe ...

"I may not be a Meta," I say. "But I'm certainly no weakling."

I go for it, darting towards the one-eyed man, but I'm quickly caught up in a tangled mass of arms and legs.

"Let me go!" I scream. But no matter how hard I push, I can't break free.

They've got me.

The woman laughs. She grabs a bottle and smashes it against the bar, leaving a sharp, jagged edge. "You shall be a warning to all of the heroes of the Freedom Force."

Then, I remember that I can stop this if I want to. All I have to do is call out GISMO's name and this nightmare will be over. But the eye-patched man grabs my head and pulls it back, exposing my neck. I try to say the words, but I can't. I can barely breathe.

The woman approaches slowly, savoring every moment. She stands in front of me and pushes the edge of the broken glass against my neck. I can feel it cutting into my skin!

I'm going to die. I'm going to die in this room for being a Zero. A stupid, freaking Zero.

"Goodbye, boy," says the woman.

I close my eyes and wait for the end.

But instead I feel a strange tickle by my ear.

Opening one eye, I see the familiar shape of a Hawk-a-rang wrapped neatly around the bottle. Then it snatches the glass clear from the woman's hand.

Can it be?

As if on cue, Shadow Hawk appears, floating down from the rafters with his long, black cape trailing behind him. He lands softly, uncurling his Hawk-a-rang. His eyes are like narrow, white slits set inside his black cowl. His lips are curled into a menacing sneer. He stares at the broken bottle and says, "Didn't your mother teach you it's not polite to hit a kid with glasses?"

"Who are you?" says the woman.

"Me?" he answers. "I'd say I'm your new problem." Shadow Hawk flexes his arm and strikes the eye-patched man with his Hawk-whip. The man cries out in pain, dumping me unceremoniously to the floor.

I land on my back and look up to see the thug holding his head. And then, something weird happens. His face starts to flicker. And, for a moment, I'm staring at something not quite human at all.

His skin turns pale orange. His one good eye molts from brown to neon green. His ears curl upwards, stopping in points beside his temples. Then he shakes his head and reassumes his human appearance.

"Get him!" the woman screams.

I look back at Shadow Hawk as the men approach, but the hero stands his ground. "GISMO," he calls. "End program."

"Training module ended, Shadow Hawk," GISMO says.

Instantly, the saloon, along with the woman and all her henchman, disappears. Shadow Hawk and I are all that remain in the plain, white room.

"Aren't you supposed to be grounded?" Shadow Hawk asks, helping me to my feet.

I nod, still trying to catch my breath.

"You realize that was an advanced combat module," Shadow Hawk says. "You should never let a simulation get so out of hand that you can get seriously hurt."

"No kidding," I say, rubbing my sore neck. "I guess I got in over my head. Sorry I was such a goober."

"A goober?" Shadow Hawk laughs. "That's not what I saw. What I saw was inexperience. Someone who doesn't yet understand his limits. But with practice you can make progress. And with progress you can get better every single day. Take it from me."

For the first time, I see Shadow Hawk in a different light. Standing before me is a member of the greatest super team ever assembled who has absolutely no Meta powers. He's a Zero, just like me, but he's pushed his mind and body to the limits of human potential. And because of that, he's probably one of the most dangerous members of the Freedom Force.

"Come on, kid," Shadow Hawk says. "Let's grab a soda pop from the Galley. Maybe I'll teach you a few things."

"Really?" I say. "You'd do that?"

"Sure," he says. "You're part of the team, aren't you?"

"Yeah," I say. "I guess so."

We walk a few steps and then I stop. "Shadow Hawk, can I ask you something?"

"Shoot, kid," he says.

"Those guys in the simulation, they weren't human, were they?"

Shadow Hawk smiles. "I was wondering if you caught that. No, they're not human. They're known as the

Skelton, an alien race of shape shifters obsessed with conquering neighboring galaxies—including ours."

We walk a few more steps.

"So, wait? You mean they're real?" I ask. "They've tried to conquer Earth?"

"Oh, they've tried," Shadow Hawk says. "Several times, in fact. But don't worry, we're the good guys. The Freedom Force has always been there to stop them."

My mind starts spinning. So, if the Skelton are real, then is that orb the woman was yammering about the same as the one the Worm had around his neck? And, if so, what did she want it for? I was about to ask Shadow Hawk, but then thought better of it. What if he thinks I'm being ridiculous? After all, he just told me not to worry about it. Besides, I have a more pressing issue to attend to.

"Shadow Hawk, can I ask one more thing?"

"Sure, kid."

"You're not going to tell my dad I was in the Combat Room, are you?"

"Nah," says Shadow Hawk. "I think you've had enough punishment for one day."

We laugh and head for the Galley.

FROM THE META MONITOR:

Meta Profile

Name: Shadow Hawk
Role: Hero   Status: Active

VITALS:

Race: Human
Real Name: Unknown
Height: 6'2"
Weight: 215 lbs
Eye Color: Unknown
Hair Color: Unknown

META POWERS:

Class: None

Powers Level:

- Meta 0
- Master detective, expert marksman, and highly-skilled martial artist.

CHARACTERISTICS:

Combat	92	
Durability	56	
Leadership	93	
Strategy	100	
Willpower	100	

SIX

I BREAK THE LAW INTO A GAZILLION PIECES

It's 10:57 p.m. and I can't stop pacing.

I'm three minutes from either getting away with my pretend new powers or going down in a massive ball of flames. My parents haven't mentioned the bank heist once since I shared my "dream" with them earlier this morning. In fact, I think they've forgotten all about it.

I glance at the Worm's mobile again. There aren't any meaningful texts since this afternoon, except for one ridiculous exchange where Brawler lost his costume. Forty-five texts later, he realized it was in the backseat of his minivan the whole time.

Freaking. Genius.

10:58 p.m.

I run my hands through my hair. This is crazy. Here I am, relying on a bunch of Meta 1 losers to hit a bank precisely at eleven o'clock so I can con my parents into believing I have Meta powers. What am I doing?

10:59 p.m.

Oh, god. What if they don't hit the bank? I'll look like a fool again. Grace will say this is just another ploy to get attention. She'll say I'm jealous of her. She'll call me pathetic. She'll recommend my parents abandon me on a deserted island and pretend I never happened. Then she'll break through our shared wall, and use my bedroom as her personal dressing room. I can see it now—the mirrors, the costumes, the hundreds of Glory Girl posters lining the walls. Boy, would she love that.

They have to hit that bank.

I peek at the phone again. Still no texts. I look back up.

11:00 p.m.

I raise my eyebrows, waiting for the Meta Monitor to sing its song. I stand silently for thirty seconds. Sixty seconds. Two minutes. But, there's nothing. Those idiots! Where are they? They were supposed to rob the bank at 11:00 p.m.!

I stare at the phone. Still no texts. What the heck are they doing? I scream in frustration and collapse on my bed. How could I ever have trusted those crooks? Grace is right. I am pathetic. Just look at me. I close my eyes and let out a deep breath. It's over. I'll never be a Meta.

Not even a sham.

"Alert! Alert! Alert!" the Meta Monitor sounds.

I spring from my bed and glance at the clock.

11:04 p.m.

"Meta 1 disturbance. Repeat: Meta 1 disturbance. Multiple signatures. Power signature one identified as Taser. Power signature two identified as Brawler. Alert! Alert! Alert!"

YEEEEEEESSSSSSSSSSSSSSSSSSS!!! They hit the bank! They hit the bank! Those idiots hit the bank!

I stop dancing and regain my composure. I run up the twenty-three steps to the Monitor Room to claim my big "I-told-you-so" moment. Luckily, Dad is on duty tonight.

"Elliott," Dad says. "I was just about to call you. Did you hear the alarm?"

"The alarm?" I say, feigning surprise. "Yes, I may have. Whatever was it for?"

"Well, Keystone Savings Bank is currently being robbed. Wasn't that your dream last night?"

"Oh, that's right," I say nonchalantly. "I had completely forgotten all about it. It was supposed to happen at eleven. Gee whiz, I forgot to look at the time. Is it eleven already?"

"You said there were three Metas, correct?" Dad asks. "The monitor is only showing two."

"Two?" I say, confused. "Did you say two? Oh, well, perhaps I was mistaken. These dreams are so hard to decipher sometimes." Where the heck is that third idiot? Now, Dad will see right through me.

"Alert! Alert! Alert! Meta 1 signature registering. Identity unknown."

"Oh, there we go," I say. "There's your third crook." Whew!

"If there's an unknown Meta, we'd better summon the whole team," Dad says. "I don't know what we're dealing with here. Did your dreams tell you anything about the third Meta?"

I can tell him the third Meta had the text handle "Makeshift," but that would just raise a lot of questions I didn't really want to answer. Better to say nothing.

"Um, no," I say. "But maybe I should come along. You know, since it was my dream and all."

Dad looks at me and smiles. "Sorry, Elliott. After the last incident, we can't risk it. But you really got me thinking. I realized that out of all of us, you're the one I admire the most."

"Me?" I say. "Why me?"

"Well, we all have responsibilities around here. Whether it's stopping a bad guy or ejecting the trash. But you have the greatest responsibility of all."

"I do?"

"*I* think so," Dad says. "Who knows more about the Freedom Force than you? Who knows all of our secret identities, the location of our secret headquarters, all of our powers and weaknesses? You do. And, you keep it locked up tight. That's a pretty big responsibility."

"Yeah, I guess," I say, kind of shell-shocked.

"Well, I want you to know that you're a big part of our family, whether you have powers or not. Remember, just having Meta powers doesn't make you a good person. Look at all of those supervillains out there. In the end, it's what's in your heart that counts, and I think you may have the biggest heart of all."

"Gee," I say. "Thanks."

"Just believe in yourself, son. You'll be amazed by what happens when you do."

"So does that mean I can come?" I ask.

"Well, no," says Dad. "We still don't have a full understanding of your powers yet. And besides, you're grounded, remember?"

"Yes, sir," I answer. "I remember." Wait, did Dad just say I had powers?

"Why don't you go back to bed and see what else you can dream about. We'll be back later. And remember, no monitor duty." He pats my head and takes off.

I'm way too wired to go back to bed. Instead, I head down to the Galley for a late-night celebratory snack.

When I arrive, I hear snoring from beneath the dining table. It sounds like Dog-Gone has snagged someone's leftovers and is invisibly sleeping it off. I open the pantry and grab the nearest non-nutritious snack I can find. I'm so pumped by what I just pulled off that I can't sit still. I decide to take my candy bar for a stroll.

Today is a massive victory. Dad is convinced I have powers. Now I just need those knuckleheads to pull off another job. Another job means another dream. And, another dream means I can continue to convince the Freedom Force that I'm a Meta. Then, I can get my own costume and go on adventures with them.

There's just one catch. I need those idiots to not get caught. I stuff the candy into my mouth, pull out the Worm's phone and type into the bank job thread:

>Worm: Hey, FF coming! Run!<

Beads of sweat drip down my forehead. Now I've sunk so low I'm actually helping the bad guys get away. Did that make me a criminal too? I'm pretty sure I know the answer to that one. But, I need them. Plus, no one's really getting hurt, are they? Now, if they'll just respond. My phone buzzes. A text from Taser:

>Taser: WHAT? Really?<

They got it! I type again:

>Worm: YES! GO! NOW!<

>Taser: Tx bro!<

Great, I'm officially a criminal.

I'm pretty sure Dad wouldn't be so proud of me now.

I look up to see where I've wandered to and, as if by some cruel twist of fate, I'm standing in front of The Vault. The Vault is the fortified chamber that stores the secret blueprints for Lockdown—the super-maximum Meta prison. The Vault is designed to be impenetrable. The door is 21-inches thick, weighs over 20 tons and is made of pure tungsten—the strongest metal on Earth. The only way in is to know the entry code, and only two people in the world know that—my dad and TechnocRat.

I study the keypad where you enter the passcode. There are nine individual spaces with only letters available, no numbers. I start working through some options in my mind.

J-U-S-T-I-C-E. Seven letters. Not enough.

L-O-C-K-D-O-W-N. Eight letters. Still short.

C-R-I-M-I-N-A-L-S. Nine letters. Maybe?

I punch it in and a red light flashes on the console with a warning. It reads:

ERROR. TWO ATTEMPTS REMAINING.

I keep thinking.

V-I-L-L-A-I-N-S. Eight letters.

P-R-I-S-O-N-E-R-S. Nine. Could be?

I type it in and up comes another warning. It reads:

ERROR. ONE ATTEMPT REMAINING.

Okay. Time to stop. Who knows what will happen if I get the last one wrong? I back away and turn around. I need to find something else to do before I get myself in even more trouble. All I need to do is just put it out of my mind. Yep, just think about something else. Something else entirely.

Well, that's not working!

The password has to be something less obvious. Think! Okay, The Vault was designed by TechnocRat. If I were TechnocRat, it would need to be something meaningful to me that I wouldn't forget. Now, what would I remember if I were a super brilliant, yet incredibly irritable rat?

Cats? No way. Secret laboratories? Definitely not. What are genius rats into these days? Super-conductors? Motherboards? Cheese? Cheese!

C-H-E-E-S-E. Six letters. Even if I added an 'S' it's only seven …

Not it.

Then it hits me. That crazy rat. Could it be?

I cross my fingers. If this doesn't work I'll either trigger an alarm that runs straight to my dad's brain or set off a booby trap that will catapult me into outer space. Out of the two, I'd definitely prefer the latter. Here goes nothing. I exhale and punch into the keypad.

C-A-M-E-M-B-E-R-T.

Nothing.

Okay, I'm officially a dead kid walking.

Suddenly, a loud BING echoes down the corridor, and the console turns green. I hear several mechanical locks rotate and unhinge from the inside. And then, to my sheer and utter delight, the door swings wide open.

I breathe a sigh of relief and step inside. The interior is much larger than it looks from the outside. There are dozens of filing cabinets all neatly organized in rows. Each cabinet has a number and name beneath it. I quickly deduce that the number must represent the corresponding prison cell number at Lockdown and the name must be the prisoner held captive inside. I move through the rows, recognizing many of the names listed as dangerous Meta 3 criminals with unbelievable powers:

Bone Crusher. Lady Killer. Gargantuan.

All locked away under one roof.

My destination, however, is the last filing cabinet. The top drawer reads:

Cell# M27 -- Meta-Taker.

I reach up and pull it open. Inside is a long tube. I take it out and twist off the cap. I unroll the blueprints onto a nearby desk and look them over.

They're the plans for Meta-Taker's cell.

There are lots of technical specifications outlining the dimensions of the cell, thickness of the walls, location of the air ventilation system and so on. What I'm most interested in, however, is located in the bottom right corner. It's the containment plan. I read it closely:

Prisoner is to be kept in a continuous state of suspended animation (otherwise known as hibernation). The temperature of the room is to be kept at 20°F (-7°C) at all times. This will keep the prisoner in a state of hypothermia. The lower body temperature will stop all cellular activity, decreasing the body's need for oxygen while keeping the cells alive. The prisoner will not have any need for food or water in this state. This containment plan replicates the hibernation pattern of animals. Room temperature is to be monitored 24 hours a day, 7 days a week.

Okay, that rat is amazing. But, I sure hope his containment plan works because I can't think of anything worse than a ticked-off Meta-Taker waking up inside a facility loaded with hundreds of Meta prisoners.

FROM THE META MONITOR:

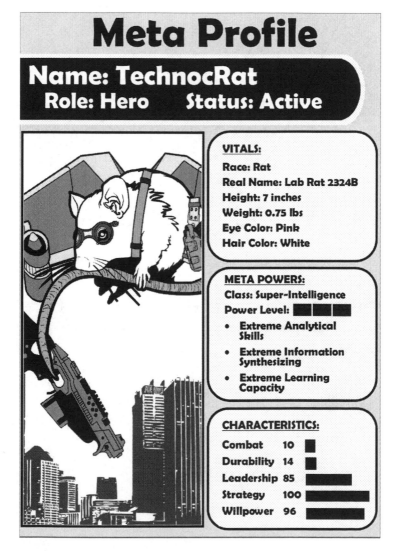

Meta Profile

Name: TechnocRat
Role: Hero   Status: Active

VITALS:

Race: Rat
Real Name: Lab Rat 2324B
Height: 7 inches
Weight: 0.75 lbs
Eye Color: Pink
Hair Color: White

META POWERS:

Class: Super-Intelligence
Power Level: ■ ■ ■
- Extreme Analytical Skills
- Extreme Information Synthesizing
- Extreme Learning Capacity

CHARACTERISTICS:

Combat   10
Durability 14
Leadership 85
Strategy   100
Willpower   96

SEVEN

I NOW WISH TO BE CALLED AWESOME BOY

So here we are, Grace and I, two kids with Meta powers heading to school via a sub-atomic teleportation device. We land at the Prop House when Grace finally blows a gasket.

"You got lucky," she says. "That's all."

"Oh, I wouldn't exactly call it luck," I say, buffing my fingernails. "Sounds like someone's upset she's no longer the only Meta kid around."

Grace turns a deep shade of purple and huffs, "It's dumb luck until you do it again."

Let's just say the ride to the Prop House was a chilly one. Grace is miffed because, apparently, everything in my "dream" came true last night. The Freedom Force arrived seconds after Taser, Brawler and the mysterious Makeshift escaped from the scene of the crime.

Then Mom and Dad spent the entire morning asking me all sorts of questions about my dreams. When did they start? Could I see people clearly in them? How did I know when they would happen in real life?

Oh, they did stop for a minute to ask Grace how she wanted her eggs. And then they turned right back to me.

Me. Me. Me.

It's shaping up to be a beautiful day.

We exit the prop house to find a surprise sitting on our front steps.

It's a girl.

"Who the heck are you?" asks Grace.

"I'm Cammie," says the girl, her bright, green eyes sparkling. "Elliot's friend."

Wait, she knows my name? And did she just say she's my friend?

"Elliott's friend?" Grace says. "Elliott doesn't have any friends."

"Shut up, Grace," I snap. "I guess you should be *walking* to school now." Grace hated to walk anywhere when she could fly. Now, because of Cammie, she's stuck.

"We'll continue this later," Grace says, her eyes throwing daggers at me. She pulls her backpack over her shoulder and storms off.

As I lock the door, it hits me that I've never really talked to a girl alone other than my sister.

We look at each other awkwardly and start walking.

"Well, she seems lovely," Cammie says.

"You have no idea," I say. "So, um, what are you doing here?"

"I pass by your house on the way to school, so I thought I'd walk with you," she says. "You know, in case you need protection or something."

I look over to see if she's serious. Her smile tells me she's not.

"Thanks," I say. "But that bully hasn't come within five-hundred miles of me since you clobbered him."

"Yeah, sorry about that," she says. "I didn't mean to step in, but... "

"No, it's okay," I say. "You did the right thing. I never did get to say thanks. So, thanks."

"No problem," she says. "I actually wasn't even sure you were home. Your lights were off the whole time. It's, like, totally dark in there."

"Oh, are they?" I say, looking back at the house. Yep, she's right, it's pitch black inside. I have to think fast. "Um, yeah, Dad gets a little crazy trying to save money on the electric bill. We're all so used to it we operate on radar now. You know, like bats." Note to self: have TechnocRat fix that asap.

Time to change the subject.

"So you're new, huh?"

"Yeah," she says. "My dad, he ... moves around a lot. I guess you could say he doesn't stay in one place for very long."

"Wow, that sounds rough," I say.

"Yeah. I don't have many friends because of it," she says. I can tell by her slumped shoulders that this makes her sad.

Is that why she was waiting for me? Maybe she knows I don't have friends either.

"You sure seem to know a lot about the Civil War," I say. "Maybe even more than Mrs. Gittes." Mrs. Gittes is our Social Studies teacher. She kind of looks like a frog, especially when she wears that green turtleneck.

"Oh, yeah," Cammie says. "I guess I like studying things like that. My dad always says it's good to learn about history so you don't end up repeating the mistakes of the past."

"Makes sense," I say. I can tell there's something more she wants to say about her father, but she doesn't. And, given my own family dynamics, I don't want to press her.

We walk in silence for a bit.

"So, what do you think about Glory Girl?" she asks.

Well, that was unexpected. I want to say: *Well, you actually just met the old sourpuss a few minutes ago after we teleported to earth.* But I think better of it. All I manage to say is, "Um ... "

"I think she's an egomaniac," says Cammie.

"You do?" I reply, my voice raising a full octave higher. I clear my throat. "I mean, you do?" I say, regulating my voice.

"Oh, please," she says. "Didn't you see her on the news last night? She made it all about her. Give me a break! I don't understand why she's all the rage. I think she should call herself Ego Girl."

"Now, that's a good one!" I snort. We just may get along after all. "So, if you're not a fan of hers, then who's your favorite hero?"

"In comic books or real life?" she asks.

"You read comic books?"

"Of course I do," she says. "They're not just for boys, you know."

"I didn't mean it like that," I clarify. "I've just never met a girl that liked comic books before. I read them all the time."

"Well, so do I," Cammie says. "And, to answer your question, my favorite comic book hero is Saturn Girl. She's pretty deadly."

"And in real life?" I ask.

"That's easy," she says. "It's Ms. Understood."

"Really?"

"Really," Cammie says. "She just seems so—down to earth. You know what I mean?"

"Oh yeah," I say. "I know."

"How about you?" Cammie asks. "Who are your favorites?"

"That's easy," I say. "In comics it's definitely Batman. And in real life—"

"Wait," Cammie interrupts, "let me guess. Shadow Hawk?"

"Hey, how'd you know that?" I ask.

"Well, it's only logical. Isn't Shadow Hawk the real-life version of Batman? He's just the smartest and most athletic man on the planet."

"Yeah," I say. "I never thought about it like that. I guess they are similar."

"And like you, they're both a bit mysterious," she adds.

I feel my cheeks flush. "You think *I'm* mysterious?"

"I think there's more to you than meets the eye, Elliott Harkness."

I'm pretty sure I'm redder than a tomato by now. Fortunately, we reach the school entrance.

"Well, it was great walking and talking with you," she says.

"Yeah, thanks for protecting me," I say. "You're like the Secret Service for sixth graders."

She laughs. "No problem. See you in Social Studies." Then she smiles and walks away.

***

School was pretty much background noise for the rest of the day. Cammie and I talked a bit in class, and she asked me if I wanted to grab a milkshake after school, but

I was still grounded. I breathed a sigh of relief when she didn't ask me why.

My luck continued after school as I also received a new stream of texts from Idiots Incorporated:

>Taser: New job. Who's in?<

>Makeshift: I'll play!<

>Demento: In.<

>Brawler: ☺ What is it?<

>Taser: Gold. Truck.<

>Brawler: They make gold trucks?<

>Taser: No u dufus! Gold arriving by truck!<

>Brawler: My bad.<

>Demento: Time?<

>Taser: Midnight.<

Flipping back through the Worm's contact list, I confirm that Demento isn't a breath mint, but rather a villain named Dr. Demento, a Meta 1 psychic. Then I see this, and my heart drops to my toes.

>Taser: U in Worm?<

>Brawler: Plus, I still have your crowbar.<

Great. Now the floodgates have opened.

I don't know what to tell them? Sorry guys, thanks for inviting me to hit the truck, but I'm actually not the Worm at all, but just a twelve-year-old kid that picked up his phone by mistake while my super-hero family was putting away some Meta creep.

I breathe in deeply and exhale.

Just relax, and cut it off quickly.

>Worm: Sorry. Prior obligation. U keep crowbar.<

Did it work? Please, please work.

>Taser: OK no prob.<

>Brawler: I can? TX! ☺☺☺<

Whew! I'm off the hook, and the Worm is short one crowbar.

After the criminals go through another exhaustive sequence of planning their crime, I have all the pertinent information. Now it's time to prove my "dreams" are more than just "dumb luck."

I wait until after dinner, and find Mom and Blue Bolt hanging out in the Galley. Here goes nothing.

"Mom, I had another dream."

"You did?" she says. "Tell me about it?"

"There were four villains," I say, "All after one truck transporting gold. Same three from the night before plus a fourth with psychic ability. It's going down at midnight."

Blue Bolt rounds up the others in a flash, and I brief them as well. The look on Grace's face is priceless.

Now all I have to do is wait.

Dog-Gone and I play the longest game of fetch known to man.

When eleven o'clock rolls around, the heroes throw me a curve ball I'm not expecting. Since the villains got away last time, the Freedom Force decide to leave early to lay a trap. My flirtation with powers is about to end prematurely.

I can't let that happen.

So, as soon as they split, I hit the texts.

>Worm: WARNING! FF setting trap!<

>Taser: WHAT? How u know?<

>Worm: Trust me.<

I wait for the inevitable text telling me the job is off. Instead I get this:

>Taser: No worries.<

Wait, what? No worries? What the heck does that mean? He must not have understood me.

>Worm: YO! I SAYS FREEDOM FORCE!!!!!<

>Taser: Yep. I SAYS NO WORRIES. ☺<

Something isn't right.

How are those morons going to stop the Freedom Force?

I start to panic. If these guys think they can take out the most powerful heroes in the universe, then they have something up their sleeves. I need to warn the Freedom Force. And, pronto!

Dog-Gone and I run up to the Meta Monitor and pull up the communication system.

"Waystation to Freedom Flyer II," I call.

There's no response, only static.

"Waystation to Freedom Flyer II," I call again.

More static.

This isn't good at all. I have to get down there. Somehow, I have to help the criminals escape while, at the same time, keep the Freedom Force from being ambushed.

I just need a way to get there.

I can't use the Transporter because there's no nearby connection. I have to find some other way. But how?

Then it hits me.

I flip to the hangar bay camera.

And there it sits, waiting for the joyride of its life.

Freedom Flyer I.

Meta Profile

Name: Blue Bolt
Role: Hero   Status: Active

VITALS:

Race: Human
Real Name: Maya Williams
Height: 5'8"
Weight: 135 lbs
Eye Color: Brown
Hair Color: Black

META POWERS:

Class: Super-Speed
Power Level: ■ ■ ■
- **Extreme Speed**
- **Enhanced Endurance**
- **Phasing through objects**
- **Super-Fast Reflexes**

CHARACTERISTICS:

Combat	86	
Durability	60	
Leadership	76	
Strategy	79	
Willpower	90	

EIGHT

I FEEL LIKE I NEED TO DIE NOW

Of all the stupid things I've done, this is probably the one most likely to get me killed. My plan was simple enough. Hijack the Freedom Flyer I, set it on auto-pilot, and swoop in to save the Freedom Force. Unfortunately, my plans usually have a way of backfiring on me.

After the infamous Master Mime-Brutal Birdmen scuffle, I knew that steering the Freedom Flyer I was going to be a challenge, but I had no idea that the auto-pilot had been junked as well. So here I am, flying a supersonic shuttle at 5,000 feet above the ground with a broken steering column, a damaged auto-pilot and no clue as to how I'm going to land this thing.

Getting the Freedom Flyer off the Waystation was no big deal. I'd played around in the computer flight simulator for so many years that I knew how to start it up and get it going. Bringing it back down, however, is another matter altogether. I never practiced landing. Flying was always the fun part.

I try several more times to get in touch with the Freedom Flyer II, but all I hear is static. There are no new texts on either my new mobile or the Worm's. I have an empty feeling in my stomach that something's wrong.

I just don't know what.

But that will have to wait because the problem with the steering column is even worse than I thought. The air is so choppy that it's constantly throwing the shuttle off course. When I pull back for more altitude the shuttle lurches to the right. I correct this by pulling the steering column down, which straightens the shuttle sometimes, but other times throws it to the left. I'm working really hard to just keep a consistent cruising speed and stay flying in one direction.

The only thing that is working is the navigation system. It's automatically synched to the Meta Monitor, which tracks any signs of Meta powers and provides the exact coordinates of their location. So, I have a pretty good read on where the action is happening. I just need to get there without overshooting it by hundreds of miles in the blink of an eye.

But, I've totally got this!

I hope.

There is one other small issue to sort out. I have no

idea what I'm going to do when I actually get there. I need to help the bad guys escape so I can continue my charade, while simultaneously ensuring that none of the good guys get hurt. Plus, my parents are absolutely going to flip out when they see me. I'm actually not sure who will kill me first.

I'm lost in thought when the Freedom Flyer chimes in, "Visual confirmation at 0300."

I zone in on the area the Freedom Flyer is signaling. There are dozens of trees felled in the same direction, as if some giant steamroller plowed them over at the roots. My eyes follow the path of destruction, stopping at a very large fire where giant plumes of black smoke billow up to the clouds. At the center of it all is a familiar object that looks like it's shattered into a million pieces.

It's the Freedom Flyer II.

Two thoughts cross my mind. One, it took something awfully powerful to do that to a Freedom Flyer. And two, I'm flying a much weaker version.

I have to locate my family and get out of there fast.

It doesn't take me long to find them.

Several miles ahead it looks like a Fourth of July celebration gone wrong. There are massive explosions everywhere accompanied by blinding flashes of light. I'm still too high to identify specific people, but I can see them all down there, scampering around like ants.

I can't shake the horrible feeling that this whole thing is my fault. I have to help, but my first job is to figure out how to safely land this thing without getting myself killed.

Apparently, someone else has other ideas.

I notice the purple energy rocket about two seconds before impact. There's no time to pull up the reflector shields. I brace myself for what is sure to be an epic collision.

I'm not disappointed.

The explosion is deafening. My head slams into the console, which can only happen if the pilot's seat I'm strapped into has completely detached from the cockpit floor. I feel woozy, like I'm floating outside my own body, but somehow stay conscious. It takes a few seconds to reorient, then I realize I'm not exactly floating, but rather free falling through the air, debris from the Freedom Flyer plunging all around me.

The good news is that I'm not dead.

The bad news is that I have seconds to act before I become the world's largest pancake.

My right hand fumbles to open the armrest and access the remote pilot touch pad. After some careful manipulation, I activate the propulsion jets mounted to the bottom of the pilot's chair. They engage and the upward thrust of the jets slows my descent. I'm safe for now, but I know there's only enough fuel to bring me to the ground. I have to find a safe place to touch down before another rocket knocks me clear out of the sky.

As I get lower, the explosions seem to be getting louder, which means I'm getting closer to the action. I try to turn, but the steering difficulties from the shuttle seem to have carried over to the chair as well. I manage to strong-arm my way to an area I think is a good distance from the fighting.

All the while, there's one detail that keeps playing over and over again in my mind.

That energy rocket was purple.

The only Meta I know that can create purple energy constructs is Master Mime.

But I don't have time to solve that one either because, as usual, things are about to get much, much worse.

"Well, well, well," came a familiar voice. "Look who decided to drop in."

My chair lands smack in front of the Worm and some other masked moron.

"And how considerate of him to bring his own front-row seat," the Worm adds. He's standing with his puny arms folded across his chest and a smug look on his face. The orb is still hanging around his neck, pulsating more rapidly than the last time I saw it.

The other guy isn't anyone I've seen before. Based on Meta profiles, I can tell he's not Taser or Brawler or Dr. Demento. He's small. Probably smaller than me. He's wearing an orange costume with a strange black and white concentric circle design. His mask covers his eyes and he has a dark mohawk and goatee. Is this Makeshift?

I try to stand up, but am held down by the seatbelt of my chair. I'm still buckled in!

"Please, don't get up on our account," the Worm says, reaching into my pocket to remove his mobile phone. "I certainly hope you enjoyed being me. I'm still not sure why you wanted to, but I'm grateful nonetheless. You see, once I realized who you were, it was child's play getting you to setup your family."

"You won't stop the Freedom Force!" I declare.

The villains laugh.

"Oh, we're not planning on stopping anybody," the Worm sneers. "We thought it would be much more entertaining to watch them stop each other."

The Worm spins my chair and what I see is so unexpected it takes my breath away.

The Freedom Force is in full-on combat with one another!

Master Mime is trying to pin down Blue Bolt with a pair of giant purple pincers. TechnocRat is chasing Shadow Hawk and Grace with a futuristic ray gun. And Mom has Dad on his knees with her mind control powers.

"Stop it!" I yell. "Make them stop!"

"What's the problem?" asks the Worm. "You've never seen your parents fight before?"

"H-How are you doing this?" I stammer.

"Now there's an interesting story," says the Worm, dropping to one knee. "Would you like to hear it?"

I nod.

"Well, you see, one night, really late, I was sitting outside my trailer, drinking a beer and feeling sorry for the pitiful state of my life, when the most incredible thing happened. Something really big fell out of the sky. Now I could tell that this 'thing' was in some serious trouble. It was covered in flames and there was a long trail of smoke. I watched the darn thing fall. It fell all the way down until it crashed into the mountains creating a huge explosion. I knew right away it wasn't a plane or a helicopter or anything ... human."

The Worm wipes his mouth. "So, I finished my beer and went into the mountains. The crash was so massive it didn't take me long to find it. There was a trail of destruction that went for miles. Anyway, I followed it until I came upon the cockpit. It was split completely in half—broken right down the middle like a cracked egg. And, you'll never guess what I found inside. Go on, guess."

"I have no idea," I say annoyed. "Enlighten me."

"The pilot. Can you believe it? The sucker was still alive, lying flat on his back. His skin was puke yellow and he had these bright green eyes and these pointy ears. He was wheezing and coughing up all this blackish-colored blood. It was disgusting. It didn't take a doctor to know he was in bad shape. Well, he looked me up and down and I could just tell that I wasn't the guy he was hoping for. But, you know what they say, 'the early Worm gets the bird.' Anyway, he was holding a box, protecting it like it was some kind of baby. He told me that it was all up to me. That I should take the box, but not to open it. Take it and hide it somewhere where *'the others'* wouldn't find it. He said the survival of the entire universe depended on it. You know what happened next?"

I shake my head.

"He died. I never found out who these 'others' were and frankly, I didn't care. You ever been given a present you weren't allowed to open? So, of course, I opened it, and inside was this little beauty." The Worm grabs the orb and starts rubbing his thumb over its smooth surface.

"I figured I could probably pawn it off. You know, get some cash and maybe retire down in Florida. But, then something weird happened. The orb started talking to me. Not out loud or anything, but inside my head. I thought I was crazy at first but ... it kept telling me that I was now the most powerful being on the planet. It kept saying it over and over and over again. I couldn't shut it up. Can you believe it? Me, a Meta 1, the most powerful being on the planet? At first, I didn't believe it either. But then, it showed me what we could do."

The Worm stares over my shoulder to where the heroes are fighting. "And then, I started to believe."

I look at the orb. Somehow it's responsible for all of this madness. The Worm is using it to control the Freedom Force! Then things start to click. The Worm had the orb when Meta-Taker appeared. The giant hole!

The Worm must have tunneled down and freed Meta-Taker so he could use the orb to control him!

And, that alien ship must have been a Skelton ship!

I needed to get that orb. I needed to take it away from him.

"Without that orb," I taunt, "you're still just a loser."

The Worm slaps me hard across the face.

"Correction," The Worm says, circling. "I *was* a loser. But aren't all Meta 1's losers by definition? Aren't we the laughingstocks of the Meta community? The misfits. The clowns. Just look at us. Gifted with all of these wonderful, but *useless* powers. So, I started thinking *what if?* What if the tables were turned?" He looks over at the heroes battling. "You wanted me to stop the fighting, didn't you?"

I nod.

"Watch this!" And then, the Worm calls out, "Stop!"

And the Freedom Force freeze in their tracks.

"Come here!" he orders.

The heroes turn and walk towards us like robots.

"Here we have the greatest heroes in the world," says the Worm. "All at my beck and call. If I say 'run,' they'll run. If I say 'attack,' they'll attack. I suppose I could keep them around. Perhaps I can use them as a Meta army of sorts? But, heroes always find a way to save the day, don't they? Nah, I think it's best if we get rid of them."

"Wait," I say. "What do you mean?"

"I mean get rid of them. Have you met my associate? He goes by Makeshift."

The little man steps forward. I knew it!

"He looks so unassuming doesn't he?" The Worm says. "Just another worthless Meta 1. Another *loser* just like me. Don't you think things would be different if there weren't so many Meta 2's and Meta 3's walking around? Shouldn't Meta 1's have a chance to be the most powerful beings on the planet?"

"Wait. What are you going to do?" I ask.

"Makeshift," The Worm says. "Get rid of 'em."

The little man steps forward and puts out his hands. "I've never done so many at once before."

"Wait!" I cry out. "Hold on!"

Suddenly, a giant yellow circle spews out from his hands and surrounds the Freedom Force. It starts to expand and contract around them, picking up more and more speed with each rotation. And then, with a giant WHOOSH, it collapses on itself, taking the Freedom Force with it.

"No!" I scream.

There's nothing left where they stood. Just patches of dirt and grass. That's it. Just dirt and grass. And, it's all my fault. I made them come here. I led them to their deaths.

The Worm comes towards me. "Now we weren't expecting you here, but it certainly helps tie up any loose ends."

He pulls a knife from behind his back.

I can try to run, but what's the point? There's nothing left. I feel tired. Woozy. Like my eyelids are tied to anchors. I feel myself giving up. Slipping into darkness. I just wanted to be part of the team.

But instead of the sharp cut of a knife, I feel a different kind of sensation; like I'm lifting into the air.

"Hey!" the Worm yells.

I look down and notice the Worm getting smaller and smaller.

I have no clue what's happening.

Then, I glance up.

For a moment, I think I see a tiny fly with bright, green eyes carrying me off into the sky.

And then, I'm out.

FROM THE META MONITOR:

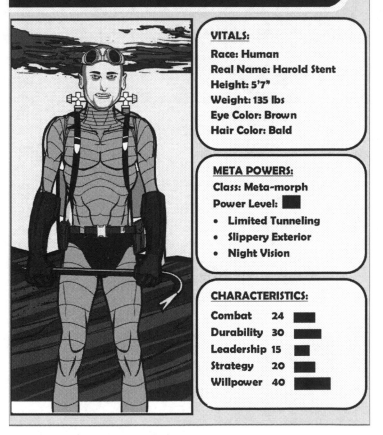

Meta Profile

Name: The Worm
Role: Villain   Status: Active

VITALS:

Race: Human
Real Name: Harold Stent
Height: 5'7"
Weight: 135 lbs
Eye Color: Brown
Hair Color: Bald

META POWERS:

Class: Meta-morph
Power Level: ▮
- Limited Tunneling
- Slippery Exterior
- Night Vision

CHARACTERISTICS:

Combat   24
Durability   30
Leadership   15
Strategy   20
Willpower   40

NINE

I GET THE SHOCK OF MY LIFE

"Elliott!"

I hear a faint noise in the distance.

"Elliott!"

Repeating itself. Getting louder. Strangely familiar.

"Elliott!"

Then, I feel a sharp smack across my cheek.

"Elliott!"

Slobber rolls down my chin.

I open my eyes. Everything is fuzzy. Blurry. But I can just barely make out the silhouette of a person standing in front of me. By the shape, I can tell it's a girl. Ever so slowly, she comes into focus. She's staring at me. Staring with these bright, green eyes. I know those eyes.

"C-Cammie? Where am I?"

I rub my cheek, which is still smarting like crazy. Did she just hit me?

I take in my surroundings. It's morning and we're in front of the Prop House. At first, I think I'm dreaming, but then I realize I'm still strapped into the pilot's chair from the Freedom Flyer I. No such luck.

"What are you doing here?" I ask.

"Don't you remember?" Cammie says. "I rescued you."

"You did what?" I say. "Rescued me from what?" I struggle to replay everything I can remember. Then it all comes flooding back: the Worm, the orb, Makeshift, my family. The fly with the bright, green... green...

My eyes lock onto Cammie's.

And then, I synthesize a million pieces of information at once.

"Y-You're the fly?" I stammer. "You were that weird fly that landed on me after the Meta-Taker fight?" I unclick myself from the pilot's seat and scramble to my feet. I feel unsteady. "Who are you? What do you want from me?"

"Oh, relax," Cammie says, rolling her eyes. "Don't you think that if I wanted to kill you I would have done it by now? Or let the Worm do it for me?"

I hesitate. "Maybe. Or, maybe you wanted to kill my family too. Just like the Worm did."

"Elliott," Cammie says. "I'm truly sorry about your family. I didn't see that coming or believe me, I would have helped. But, I also know what it's like to lose someone you love. You see, the Worm confirmed my deepest fears. My father is dead."

Her father? What is she talking about?

And then, I realize what she means. That alien that crash landed on Earth with the orb. It feels like someone dumped a bucket of ice down my shirt.

"Your father was a Skelton!" I blurt out. "So, that means..." Instinctively, I move behind the pilot's chair.

She smiles. "Guilty as charged." And then, before my eyes, she transforms from the girl I know as Cammie to an alien version of herself. Her eyes brighten from emerald to neon green. Her skin takes on a pale, yellow hue. Her ears climb upwards, stretching to her temples. Her clothes transform from preppy to … regal. Her white top and skirt are adorned with gold trim, and thick, gold jewelry surrounds her neck and wrists. "My birth name is K'ami Sollarr," she says, her tone turning much more formal. "I am the daughter of the Chief Scientist of the Skelton Empire. Or, at least, I was."

All of the horrible things Shadow Hawk told me about the Skelton pop into my brain. "You're evil. You're here to take over the Earth."

"No, Elliott," she says. "I'm not here to take over the Earth. I'm here to save it."

"Yeah, right," I say, mapping out escape routes.

"Tell me," she says. "Are all humans the same? Do you share the same beliefs as the Worm?"

"No," I answer. "That's ridiculous."

"It is, isn't it?" K'ami says. "Yet, you stand here accusing me of the same thing. You must understand that just as all humans are not the same, neither are all Skelton. There are those that exist only to conquer, but there is a brave minority of us that believe there is another path. My father was one of those. That is why he stole the Orb of Oblivion."

"The orb of what?"

"The Orb of Oblivion," K'ami says, "It is a cosmic parasite of sorts, a sentient object of dark matter that seeks out unfulfilled desires and feeds off of them to make itself stronger. Its powers are as expansive as the imagination of its host."

"So you're saying that this orb is feeding off the Worm?"

"Yes," she says. "And, it is getting stronger by the day."

"So, how do you know so much about this ... Orb of Oblivion? How do I know you're not making this whole thing up?"

K'ami lowers her head. "As you have alluded to, my people are conquerors—destroyers—always looking for more influential ways to expand our Empire. We have spent centuries looking for the Orb of Oblivion. Some thought it was only a legend—a fantasy told to small children. But, the Emperor believed it was real. He demanded that every inch of the universe be searched and catalogued in his quest to find it. Many thought it was a fool's quest. Until one day, it wasn't."

K'ami looks up to the sky. "A strange signal was picked up on the far side of a desolate galaxy. It was determined that the signal had come from the implosion of a large star. Our calculations had not predicted its demise, and our scientists could offer no justification. It was determined that something unnatural had happened. So a squadron was deployed to investigate. After many cycles, they had all but given up identifying a cause when a final reconnaissance drone made a remarkable discovery. It was an orb. It was lying on the surface of an unnamed moon orbiting a barren planet. No one knew how it had gotten there. Yet, there it was."

She pauses. I notice her voice has lowered and she's clenching her fists.

"It was brought back to Skelton. Naturally, as Chief Scientist, my father had the task of confirming that the orb was legitimate. He was a good man of extraordinary intellect and integrity. One night, he came to my room. It seemed as if the weight of the universe was on his shoulders. He sat for a long time in silence. And then he told me that the orb was talking to him. That every time he touched it, it would tell him to do dangerous things. When I asked what he meant, he would not say."

"We sat in silence for a while longer. And then he told me that the orb did not find itself on that little moon by accident. Somebody had put it there—far, far away where no one would ever find it. Then, he said something even more remarkable. He told me that the Orb of Oblivion had orchestrated its own freedom. That somehow, the orb had convinced that star to explode so it would emit a light so bright it would shine across the galaxy. So it could be found. My father wondered aloud that if an object of such power could convince a star to explode, then what would it be capable of doing in the hands of a Skelton Emperor? We both knew what he had to do. He made me promise him that I would be strong—that I would never show weakness. That is the last time I saw him."

"So he stole the orb and brought it to Earth?" I ask. "Thanks a lot."

"My father was a man of peace," K'ami says. "His landing on Earth was not his fault. It was mine."

"What?"

"You see, on our world, blood lines share a powerful bond. A direct psychic link of sorts. My father had arranged to hide me with friends he had trusted, but after he left they betrayed him. I was turned over to the Emperor. I was ... tortured. They exploited my psychic connection to track my father down. Somewhere deep in space they caught up with him. After a terrible battle, he prevailed, but his ship was badly damaged. Earth was the closest planet to land and try to recuperate. It was then that he disconnected from me. I had betrayed him. I waited for him to reach out to me again, but he never did.

I feared he was dead, but I had to know for sure. Now I do."

Tears well up in her eyes.

"I'm sorry," I say.

"After that, I expected they would kill me," K'ami says. "It was their mistake that they did not. I conserved my strength and waited for the right moment. When that moment arose, I struck. I stole a supply ship and followed my father's path to Earth. I swore that I would finish what he started. I had just enough fuel to make the journey. As soon as I landed on your planet, I could sense the immense power of the orb. It was palpable, as if it was calling out to me. I followed it to its source. And that's when I discovered you."

"Me?" I say. "What do I have to do with all of this?"

"You, Elliott Harkness, are the savior of the universe."

"What?" I say. "Are you nuts? If you knew anything about me you'd know that I pass out in the face of danger." I start to inch towards the Prop House. "Look, I'm really sorry about your dad, but right now I just want to go up to my room, curl up into a little ball and never come out."

Then something unusual catches my eye.

The door to the Prop House is ajar.

We never left the door unlocked, let alone open. Never. Ever. Ever.

"What is wrong?" K'ami asks.

I push the front door. It swings open with a creepy screech. Although it's dark inside, I can tell immediately that something isn't right. I turn on the lights.

At first, it looks like the house has been robbed. Tables and chairs are turned over, bookshelves are emptied, the television is smashed, pictures shattered. Then I realize, this is no burglary. Everything is still here, although now completely destroyed.

Whoever did this wasn't looking to steal anything.

They were looking for something.

My eyes immediately zoom to the end table. The miniature model of the Statue of Liberty is lying on its side, the giant mirror nearby is cracked from top to bottom. I feel short of breath. Someone has found the Transporter.

Then I remember Dog-Gone.

"I've got to go!" I say, rushing inside.

"I will go with you," K'ami says, quickly following behind.

I pull the statue and the giant mirror slides up into the ceiling. Behind it is the Transporter. If it's damaged in the slightest, my atoms could be transferred to Pluto! It looks fine, but then again, I don't know the first thing about teleportation tube maintenance. There's no doubt this could backfire in a big way.

"What is this primitive device?" K'ami asks, looking inside.

"It's a teleporter," I answer. "It transmits to our secret headquarters in space. Look, I appreciate you saving me and all, but I can't guarantee this thing still works. So if you want to back out now, I'll completely understand."

"Elliott Harkness," K'ami says with a look of utter disbelief. "Do you really think that after being captured, tortured, and escaping from the clutches of the Skelton Empire that I'm going to let a potential sub-atomic mix-up scare me away?"

"Um, right," I shrug. "Okay then, let's go."

We enter the chamber and the door closes behind us. We watch the overhead console move from red to green. Although my stomach starts to get that funny feeling as the Transporter does its thing, my mind is racing trying to figure out who ransacked the Prop House and, more importantly, what might be waiting for us on the other side.

In a few seconds we're going to find out, ready or not. The console moves back to green and the doors pop open. K'ami and I jump out prepared for the fight of our lives.

Except, there's nothing.

The room is empty. It's eerily silent. I hoped Dog-Gone would be there to greet us. Unless he's here already, but invisible.

"Dog-Gone," I whisper.

But there's no response. I start walking around the room, feeling underneath the tables to ensure he isn't hiding. Or sleeping. Or worse.

"What are you doing?" K'ami whispers back.

I realize that K'ami doesn't know about Dog-Gone, and because of that, I probably look like a crazy person. I decide that I'll keep him as my little secret for now. Just in case she turns on me.

"Um, nothing," I answer. "Just looking for a blaster or something. C'mon, let's go." Not finding Dog-Gone makes me very, very nervous.

We exit the Transporter and head for the Meta Monitor. I can just sense that someone's up here.

"Welcome home," comes a voice dripping with malintent.

Sitting on the bottom stair is a skinny, masked man. He's wearing a green costume with two white lightning bolts that start at each shoulder and meet in the middle of his chest. His hair is white and spikey, like he just stuck a knife in a toaster. I know immediately that it's Taser!

I turn to escape, only to find an enormous brute filling the entranceway behind us. His head seems way too small for his massive frame. He's wearing a burglar mask and a costume with giant spikes on his shoulders. Brawler!

"The Worm thought you might try to go home," says Taser. "Nice digs you got here. It's a little out of the way for pizza delivery, but I could get used to it."

"What are you doing here?" I ask.

"We need to get into Lockdown," Brawler says.

"Shut up, you big lug," Taser barks. "It's none of your business, kid."

"Sorry," says Brawler, looking like he dropped his ice cream cone in the dirt.

"Why do you need to get into Lockdown?" I ask. There are only two reasons I can think of as to why a criminal would want to be within a mile of the place: to kill someone inside or break someone out.

"Well, now that the cat's out of the bag, word on the street is that you've got all the blueprints up here," Taser says. "Pretty clever, but now that we're all together I suggest you make this easy and tell us where they're stashed. Otherwise," he says, "things may get a little rough for you and your weirdo girlfriend."

"K'ami," I whisper, "Turn into a fly. Save yourself."

"No Elliott. I am staying with you."

"Now, what say we make this easy?" Taser says.

"What say you shove it!" I shoot back.

"So that's how it's going to be, huh?" says Taser. "You heard him then, fellas. Waste 'em."

The villains start to close in, but there's nowhere for us to go.

We're trapped.

FROM THE META MONITOR:

Meta Profile

Name: Taser
Role: Villain   Status: Active

VITALS:

Race: Human
Real Name: Calvin Sharpe
Height: 5'11"
Weight: 170 lbs
Eye Color: Blue
Hair Color: White

META POWERS:

Class: Energy Manipulation
Power Level: ▮

- **Limited Generation of Electric Volts**
- **Immune to Electricity**

CHARACTERISTICS:

Combat	51	▬▬▬
Durability	32	▬▬
Leadership	24	▬
Strategy	31	▬▬
Willpower	40	▬▬

TEN

I LIED, NOW I GET THE SHOCK OF MY LIFE

"Elliott Harkness, use your powers!" K'ami yells, pressing back to back with me.

I'm now staring down Brawler, who's filling the doorway behind us with his ginormous muscles, while she faces Taser, who's blocking the stairs and gearing up to unleash an up-close-and-personal display of pyrotechnics.

"What are you talking about?" I say. "I don't have powers."

"Use them," K'ami orders. "Now!"

"I don't know what you're talking about!" I scream back.

Then, I hear a crackling noise. I peer over my shoulder and see electric volts leaving Taser's fingers. They're white and stringy and heading straight for K'ami.

I expect her to get out of the way, but she doesn't move. Without thinking, I pull her by the elbow and wheel around in front of her. I feel an intense, burning sensation on my chest, and then the currents arc over my head and strike Brawler square in the face, stopping the big man in his tracks.

"Ouch," Brawler says. "That hurt!" He's clearly dazed, but tries to take another step. Then his massive muscles start contracting violently. "W-W-W-Why d-d-did you hurt m ... " His eyes roll back in his head, and he comes toppling down with a tremendous thud. His body convulses on the floor for several more seconds before stopping.

He doesn't move again.

I look down at my chest. My shirt is singed black, but it's like the volts never even touched me. I look up to find everyone staring at me with their jaws hanging open. Everyone that is, except for one.

"Well done, Elliott Harkness," K'ami says. "Now it is my turn." Then she morphs into a fly and makes a beeline for Taser, hitting him with such force that he smacks his head against a stair tread and lands in a crumpled heap. But, before he can rise, K'ami is on him like a winged whirlwind, landing blow after blow until Taser's eyes go white and he's down for the count.

It's over.

"Impressive," came a nasally voice. "But you're still

going to die."

I spin to find a small man stepping out of the shadows. He's got an egg-shaped head, dark glasses, and wears a doctor's coat over his green, surgical scrubs.

It's Dr. Demento! He's a Meta 1 psychic, which means that he's about to throw a royal mind-bender our way! There's no time to react!

I brace myself, when suddenly, Dr. Demento is slammed from behind with incredible force. He flies forwards, hitting his head against the underside of the stairwell and falling to the ground unconscious.

Just then, Dog-Gone appears in front of me, his tail wagging.

I wrap my arms around him. "Good boy! I'm so happy to see you." He licks my face over and over. I feel tears sliding down my cheeks, because I realize this fleabag is all the family I have left.

As K'ami glides over, Dog-Gone begins to growl.

"Can this creature be trusted?" she asks, returning to her natural appearance.

"I think he's wondering the same thing," I answer, shielding my face as I wipe the tears away. "Why did you just stand there when Taser attacked? You could have been killed."

"But you did not let that happen," she replies. "Did you?"

"Well, no," I say. "I wasn't going to sit back and let you fry."

"Just as I had hoped," she says. "If you are going to save the universe, you must show no weakness."

"Universe, shmooniverse," I say, feeling my chest. I look down my shirt to see if I'm injured, but there are no marks on my skin. "Why didn't I turn into toast back there?"

"I was hoping you would tell me," K'ami says. "After all, it was you who did it."

"That's the thing," I say. "I don't know what I did or how I did it. The volts hit my shirt, but then they just sort of bounced right over me. They never even touched my body. What kind of power is that anyway?"

"All I can offer is an account of what I have witnessed," K'ami says. "When I came upon you during the Meta-Taker battle you were in a dire situation. Naturally, I thought the beast was going to destroy you. But, to my surprise, he did not. When he tried to explore your powers there was something deep inside of you that neutralized his, if only for a moment. Of course, at the time you did not realize that Meta-Taker was being controlled by the Worm or that, in turn, the Worm was being controlled by The Orb of Oblivion. So, when Meta-Taker sensed your powers, I heard something I never imagined I would hear in a million lifetimes."

"And what was that?" I ask.

"I heard the Orb scream," she says.

"Um, you heard it do what?" I say.

"I know it may seem strange," she continues. "But I

realized upon landing on Earth, that I had a psychic connection with the Orb. And, although the connection was weak, it was true. Somehow, I could sense its presence. At first, this surprised me. I could not understand how it could be so. But then I came to make sense of it. You see, the Orb had a direct psychic bond with my father, and my father had a direct psychic bond with me. So, by this association, the Orb and I are connected. I would not say the bond we share is strong, but it is there. It is through this connection that I was able to track down the Orb and find you. And, that is how I learned a most surprising thing."

"Oh, joy," I say. "I can't wait to hear this one."

"Elliott Harkness, the Orb of Oblivion is afraid of you."

"What?" I laugh. "It's afraid of me? You're freaking nuts."

"You are the only one capable of capturing it."

"Riiight," I say. "Well, you'll have to tell the Orb to get in back of the line, because the only thing I'm interested in capturing right now is the jerk who offed my family."

"Alert! Alert! Alert!" the Meta Monitor blares. "Meta 1 disturbance. Power signature identified as the Worm. Alert! Alert! Alert!"

"Speak of the devil," I say, starting for the Meta Monitor. But then, I realize we can't just leave these losers lying around. I run to the Equipment Room and grab some industrial-strength cable. In no time, we tie them up.

"Dog-Gone," I say, "Can you drag these guys into the utility closet and lock them inside?"

He looks at the massive size of Brawler and then back at me. He cocks an ear.

"Dog-Gone," I start, "Don't even think about—"

Then he turns invisible.

Yep, you can't teach an old dog new tricks. But, I don't have time to negotiate.

"Look," I say firmly, "if you get all these guys locked up, I'll give you the entire darned bag of doggie treats. Deal?" I can only imagine the mess that's going to be waiting for me if I survive this thing.

Dog-Gone becomes visible, his tail wagging.

"Good," I say. "And, be quick about it. If any of them wake up before you get them inside, the deal's off."

Dog-Gone licks his lips, and starts dragging Brawler by the foot.

I turn to K'ami. "Follow me."

I lead her up the stairwell and into the Monitor Room. The screens are flashing on Meta 1 alert. I hop into the command chair and take control of the keyboard. After a few commands, I pinpoint the location of the Worm.

He's at Lockdown, just as Taser said he'd be. But what did he want the escape plans for? Every horrible villain on the planet is residing there. Who's he trying to free? Could it be Meta-Taker again? Or Black Cloud? Then I flash back to something he had said in reference to the

Freedom Force: *Perhaps I could use them as a Meta army of sorts.*

Then a strange thought crosses my mind.

What if he wants to free *all* the villains?

O ... M ... G... !

"K'ami," I say, "how powerful did you say the Orb was again?"

"As I had mentioned," she says. "The power of the Orb is limited only by the imagination of its host."

"Yep, that's what you said." I realize that the Worm may be far more imaginative than I hoped. It appears that stopping the Orb has now jumped to job number one. And, lucky me, apparently I'm the only person in the entire freaking universe who can do it.

I turn to K'ami. "Okay, so how am I supposed to capture the Orb exactly? Is there some instruction manual or something you're keeping from me? Or, do I just yank it off the Worm's scraggly little neck?"

"Unfortunately, it will not be that easy," says K'ami. "If you touch the Orb directly it will try to take control of your mind. We cannot risk this. Instead, we must find the Shield Box."

"What's a Shield Box?" I ask.

"Before my father left Skelton, he told me that he had built a special containment box to house the Orb. He called it a Shield Box. I do not know what it was made of, but I do know that it was effective in keeping the Orb from direct skin contact while also shielding my father from its psychic control. If we can locate the Shield Box, we have a chance at capturing the Orb of Oblivion."

Then I remember something the Worm said. About how the alien had given him a box and the Worm had opened it and ...

"I know where the box is!" I say.

I start punching into the keyboard.

The Worm's profile pops up on the screen.

"The Worm told me he saw your father's spaceship crash to Earth from outside his trailer. So he lives in a trailer park. And, he said the ship crashed in the mountains. So, his trailer park must border a mountain range." I triangulate the Worm's last four weeks' worth of Meta 1 signatures with the locations of all the trailer parks in the country and their proximity to any mountain ranges. Then I let the Meta Monitor do its work. One minute later a set of coordinates appears.

Bingo! Grant City Trailer Park. Sixty-three miles west of the Prop House.

"That is his home?" K'ami asks.

"Yes," I say. "But, both of the Freedom Flyer shuttles are trashed. We can take the Transporter down to Earth, but after that I don't have a way for us to get there. Maybe we can hitchhike or something?"

K'ami shakes her head disappointingly. "Elliott Harkness, did you forget already?" she says, transforming into a fly. "I have already carried you over one-hundred miles to get us here. What is sixty-three more?"

FROM THE META MONITOR:

Meta Profile

Name: Brawler
Role: Villain   Status: Active

VITALS:

Race: Human
Real Name: Duncan Meeks
Height: 6'5"
Weight: 350 lbs
Eye Color: Brown
Hair Color: Black

META POWERS:

Class: Super-Strength
Power Level: ■

- Limited Strength
- Limited Invulnerability
- Limited Earthquake-Stomp

CHARACTERISTICS:

Combat	68	■■■■
Durability	65	■■■■
Leadership	5	▌
Strategy	8	■
Willpower	27	■■

ELEVEN

I ATTEND AN ALIEN FUNERAL

We leave Dog-Gone to his job, with an advance payment of ten doggie treats—just to be safe. Then, we return to Earth via the Transporter.

I strap myself back into the pilot's seat and then K'ami hauls me sixty-three miles over land and sea without taking a single break. Talk about super fly! Although we cruise along at a good clip, I'm able to get K'ami to answer a few questions that are "bugging" me, so to speak.

First, I learn that all Skelton are shape shifters. Their genetic makeup is so close to human biology that it's easy for them to morph into human form. However, transforming into a species with a totally different genetic profile is far more difficult. Most Skelton can only morph into one or two of these other species. Occasionally, a Skelton is born with the rare ability to transform into an unlimited number of forms, but they're taken from their families at birth to be trained as part of an elite killing force. According to K'ami, the name of this death squadron translates roughly into English as "Blood Bringers." That sure doesn't sound like a glee club.

Next, I learn that K'ami's particular shape, the fly, is a more well-traveled pest than I imagined. Flies first made their way to Skelton thousands of years ago as stowaways on scout ships that had visited Earth. Given K'ami's incredible strength while in fly form, they've clearly undergone some improvements since then. But otherwise, their contributions to Skelton society remained similar to their earthen cousins. On both planets, they typically end up beneath someone's shoe.

Finally, I dig in a little deeper about this Skelton Emperor. After all, if this guy had been searching for years to find the Orb of Oblivion I have a sinking feeling he's not just going to fold up the shop and give up on it. And surprise, surprise, the Emperor is not a very nice fellow. As Skelton history goes, he was originally eighteenth in line to ascend the throne, but he murdered his parents and siblings to claim the crown. Then he proceeded to dispose of anyone he thought would oppose him, starting with their heads and working downwards. He rules his world with an iron fist and believes there can be only one master of the universe which, of course, he thinks ought to be him.

So, the two-part plan is simple.

First, we need to get the Orb of Oblivion. And second, we have to get it the heck off of Earth as quickly as possible. But, I'll have to figure *how* we'll actually be doing this later, because we finally find her father's ship.

Or should I say, what's left of it.

For the last several miles we've been tracking debris from the crash, we saw bits and pieces here and there, but as we continued to follow the trail the debris was in much larger chunks. When we finally reach the heart of the scene, I feel K'ami shudder. I can't blame her. The magnitude of the destruction is unreal.

It appears that upon impact the ship burrowed itself deep into the face of the mountain, like some massive gravy divot in a heap of mashed potatoes. And, just as the Worm described, the cockpit is chopped completely in half. You couldn't have split it more evenly if you had used a chainsaw.

We descend smoothly to the ground, landing smack in the middle of the compartment halves. As I unbuckle myself from the chair, K'ami changes back to her natural form. I see tears in her eyes, but she wipes them away quickly and regains her composure.

"We must find the Shield Box," she says.

I nod in agreement, but I'm not sure the worst is over. From what the Worm told me there's a body around here somewhere. Her father's body.

K'ami heads for one half of the cabin. I search the other.

I enter my side of the cockpit, and what I find astounds me. Every inch of the interior is lined with buttons, switches and monitors of all different shapes and sizes. There are alien markings all over the place that I can't begin to understand. Towards the front of the ship's nose is a pilot's seat and some sort of helmet that's connected to the roof by a thin cable. I climb inside and take a seat in the chair. I can only imagine what TechnocRat would have thought about all this advanced technology. He'd probably memorize every detail and have it replicated within the hour. Boy, I miss that rat.

Without thinking it through, I reach up, grab the helmet suspended above me, and pull it onto my head.

There's a loud whirring noise and then all the monitors flick on. Red lights begin flashing all over the place. I have a sneaking suspicion I've done something incredibly stupid.

"Stop!" K'ami says, charging in and ripping the helmet off my head.

"Ouch," I say, rubbing my noggin. That's going to leave a mark. "Sorry. I didn't know that was going to happen."

"Skelton warships operate by sentient control," she says. "Unless you are intending to send a personal invitation for the Emperor to join us, then I suggest you refrain from touching anything you do not fully understand. Is that clear?"

"Crystal," I answer, sliding off the chair. "Did you ... find anything?"

K'ami pauses for a moment and then looks down. "Yes."

I feel terrible for her. Although my family is gone, I didn't face the harsh reality of seeing them dead. In some strange way, I feel lucky. "Then we should give him a proper burial."

She nods.

I touch her shoulder and exit the cockpit. Immediately upon entering the other side I find his body on the floor. He's lying face up, his eyes wide open and his arm propped up against the console like he's hoping someone will help him stand up. His clothes are covered in dried, black blood. It looks like he suffered a slow, agonizing death.

It's strange seeing the body of a man—an alien man— that I've never met before, but know so much about. I step outside and find a piece of wreckage I can use as a shovel and begin digging a large hole. K'ami sits nearby, facing the mountains. I work slowly, giving her time with her thoughts. It takes a while to get the hole deep enough, but when I'm ready, we lift her father's body and place it inside.

K'ami bows her head and begins the ceremony. "It is tradition to return a noble Skelton man to the soil from which he came. Though we are far from home, my father,

R'and Sollarr, gave proof that his was a soul that could not be confined to the soil of just one world. By his brave actions, this world, and all worlds known and unknown, owe him an eternal debt of gratitude. Father, I pledge that I will finish what you have started. Strength be with you in your eternal journey. Never show weakness."

As day turns to night, we bury him and mark his grave with a large rock.

When we're done, we rest under the starry sky.

"Those villains back at your headquarters mentioned they were looking for blueprints for a place called Lockdown," she says. "What is this Lockdown?"

"Oh, yeah," I say. I debate holding the secret back from her, but I have nothing to lose. At this point it's us against the world. "I guess I should connect the dots for you. Lockdown is a super-maximum jail that holds our most dangerous Meta-powered criminals. We keep the designs for their containment cells on the Waystation."

"And how do you keep these prisoners confined?" she asks. "Won't they just break out? Like the Meta-Taker, how do you keep someone like him confined?"

So I explain all the details of Lockdown and how Meta-Taker's cell works. She tells me there once was a prison moon orbiting Skelton where they sent all of their criminals. One day it was taken over by the prisoners, and all the guards were taken hostage. But instead of negotiating with the criminals to free the captives, the Emperor simply blew up the entire moon, loyal subjects and all. If that's a preview of things to come I'm far from comforted.

We sit in silence for a while.

Then she says, "I thank you, Elliott Harkness. I thank you for everything. What do you say on your planet? Now we are BFs?"

"No, K'ami," I smile back. "It's called BFFs. And yes, I feel the same."

She brushes a strand of hair from her face. It's hard to tell from her alien complexion, but I think she's blushing.

"I guess we should try to find the Shield Box?" I say, quickly changing the subject. "The Worm says he didn't take it with him, so it must be around here somewhere."

"But where?" K'ami says.

"I don't know," I mutter. "Where would you be hiding if you were a Shield Box?"

"What did you say?" K'ami says, snapping to attention.

"Me?" I say. "Nothing. It's just an expression. You know, like, if you were a Shield Box, where would you be?"

"That's it!" K'ami says.

"That's what?"

"The Shield Box," she says. "It must not be *just* a box! It's alive!"

"What is it with you aliens and everything being alive?" I ask.

"You do not understand. On the red moon orbiting Skelton lives a rare creature with remarkably dense skin.

Every cycle, each of these creatures produces a gem that is highly valued on our planet. They bury themselves in the ground until they are ready to hatch. When they climb to the surface, they are harvested for their bounty. Then, they dig back underground and do it all over again."

"You mean, like an oyster?" I say.

"Somewhat," she says, standing up. "They are large, simple organisms, impervious to any form of stimulation: electricity, fire, water ... and, apparently, mind control. On our world they are known as Sheelds."

I'm still confused.

"On your world," says K'ami, "they would be spelled S-H-E-E-L-D-S."

"Wait a minute," I say. "So this S-H-I-E-L-D Box we've been looking for is really an S-H-E-E-L-D Box? Made of one of these alien thingies?"

"Yes," she says. "I am certain of it. It is here, but it has probably buried itself somewhere." K'ami drops to her hands and knees. "Help me look."

I join her and together we comb through every inch of rock surface surrounding the wreck, but can't turn up anything. When we finish, we're completely spent. There's no sign of it anywhere on the mountain. It seems hopeless.

Then my eyes drift back to the cockpit, and I have a flash of inspiration.

"Can these things dig through stuff harder than rock?" I ask.

"I suppose so," K'ami says. "They operate purely on instinct. If they are frightened they would burrow through anything to reach safety."

"Right," I say. "The Worm told me he opened the box right when he got his grubby little hands on it."

"Do you think?" K'ami says.

"Follow me." And, I lead her back into the cockpit where we found her father.

We look down and, sure enough, there it is. A round hole cut straight through the metal of the ship and into the underlying rock. Right beneath the area her father was lying. We missed it.

K'ami kneels down and starts scooping out metal shards and loose dirt. After a few minutes, she reaches in elbow-deep and pulls out a strange looking object that's slightly bigger than her palm. It's square and brown with a thick, rippled hide. If you weren't paying attention, you could easily mistake it for a leather box.

"That's a Sheeld?" I ask.

"Yes," she says. "This is a Sheeld."

"And it's alive?" I say.

K'ami tickles it's underside and it opens up, revealing its fleshy, red interior. "Yes," she says. "Thankfully."

Then I notice something strange stuck to the roof of its mouth. It looks like a small, blue disc.

It's pulsating.

"What's that?" I ask.

K'ami peers inside and her expression turns dark. She

grabs the disc and crushes it in her hand.

"What is it?" I ask.

"A Skelton tracking device," K'ami says. "The Blood Bringers are coming."

FROM THE META MONITOR:

Meta Profile

Name: K'ami Sollarr
Role: Hero   Status: Active

VITALS:

Race: Skelton
Real Name: K'ami Sollarr
Height: 5'0"
Weight: 100 lbs
Eye Color: Green
Hair Color: Black

META POWERS:

Class: Meta-morph
Power Level: ■■
- Considerable Shape-Shifting
- Considerable Flight, Strength and Speed in Fly form.

CHARACTERISTICS:

Combat	75	
Durability	45	
Leadership	36	
Strategy	73	
Willpower	75	

TWELVE

I GO STRAIGHT TO THE SLAMMER

So here's the situation. On the one hand, we have a Meta 1 villain armed with the most powerful weapon in the universe trying to take over the world. On the other, we have a group of psycho extra-terrestrials speeding to Earth to destroy it. And somehow, stuck in the middle of it all, with the fate of the entire galaxy hanging in the balance, is an alien fly-girl and yours truly.

It certainly doesn't inspire confidence.

After much heated debate, K'ami and I finally agree that we can only deal with one twisted reality at a time. And, since the Blood Bringers haven't even shown up yet, that leaves us with one viable option. So, we hightail it to Lockdown to take out the Worm.

The place looks exactly as I remember it.

By day, it's the most impressive prison facility in the world. By night, it's the keeper of nightmares.

As we approach, it's hard not to feel like ants marching towards an elephant. First, we're greeted by a fifty-foot perimeter wall that's smothered in razor wire and motion sensors. We follow the wall until we reach the front gates—massive structures forged from impenetrable tungsten steel. Guard towers are stationed every twenty feet outfitted with spotlights and ground-to-air machine guns. Inside the perimeter, the main building rises like a steel octopus, soaring hundreds of feet high with eight separate wings sprouting out like tentacles.

I'd visited Lockdown once before to drop off Dad's lunch after he had accidentally left it at home. I was so freaked out I didn't go any farther than the front gates. This time I won't be so lucky.

Well before we'd even reached the gates, I noticed a few things that set my spine tingling. First, there's no one around. Normally, the place is swarming with guards, maintenance workers and hundreds other people. But at the moment, the prison looks like a ghost town. And as disconcerting as that is, unfortunately, it's not the most disturbing thing. That distinction goes to the front gates themselves, which are currently sitting wide open. Typically, you'd need a Meta 4 assault to get inside the place. But today, the prison seems to be inviting us in. And, I'm pretty sure neither of us thinks that's a good thing.

I turn to K'ami, her face a picture of determination.

"What do you think?" I ask.

"The Orb is here," she says. "I sense it."

"Then it's up to us," I say. "Never show weakness."

"Never show weakness," she agrees.

We step through the gates and head for the main building. We move warily, our eyes darting about the compound for signs of life, but there's nothing.

A few minutes later we reach the main building. The doors are closed. A sign on the building reads:

Stop! Extreme Danger! Official Access Only.

I turn the door handle and push. The door swings open. It all seems way too easy.

It seems like a trap.

I can tell Kami's thinking the same thing. But, what other choice do we have? She nods and we go inside.

The hallway is dark and narrow. Small sconces line the walls, providing enough light to see only a few feet in front of us before we are swallowed up into darkness. The hum from the air conditioning system provides a steady stream of white noise, accompanied by freezing cold air. K'ami shivers and crosses her arms.

"What now?" I ask.

"Now," she says, "we go forward."

On our left we pass a doorway to the main control room. Through a skinny window we see several computer stations and monitoring kiosks. All of them are unmanned.

The hallway veers left before presenting another set of doors. A sign above reads:

Meta Wing M: Meta-morphs. Official Access Only.

A half-smashed security interface is dangling from the wall, and when I push on the doors, they open without triggering an alarm.

We step inside.

The light is somewhat brighter here, but it's still kind of dim. It's clear we've entered another long and narrow corridor, only this one is flanked by dozens of cells. Some of the cell doors have windows and others don't. Cell numbers are displayed prominently above each door and a small sign hangs to the right of each doorway.

We move down the hall.

The cells seem to be grouped by Meta class, starting with the Meta 1's. All the cells are closed, and I can see through the doors with windows that their respective residents are still locked up inside.

I read the signs as we move past. It's like a "Who's Who" of the evil and notorious:

Cell# M3: Pliable Pete — Meta 1. Can contort body into various shapes. Beware: may disguise self as food tray or utensil to procure exit.

Cell# M5: Amphibia — Meta 1. Can transform into water form. Beware: may float upside down to fake own death.

Cell# M7: Double Trouble — Meta 1. Can split into two identical beings. Beware: may instigate fight with self to cause false distraction.

We then hit the Meta 2 section. The precaution language gets more serious.

Cell# M11: Pois-Anne — Meta 2. Poison kiss can paralyze. Warning: may fake need for mouth to mouth resuscitation.

Cell# M13: Mud Monster — Meta 2: Body is made of chemically altered mud. Warning: may try to sneak parts of body out as mud stains on clothing or bottom of shoes.

Cell# M17: The Phantom Raider — Meta 2: Can turn invisible. Warning: may appear not to be in cell, but trust us—he's in there.

It's too quiet. I can sense that something's just waiting to trip us up. Then we reach the Meta 3 section, and my heart skips a beat.

Every cell door is busted open.

Every. Freaking. One.

I quickly skim the signs:

Cell# M21: Flameout — Meta 3: Can transform into a being of pure fire. Danger: do not enter under any circumstance! No smoking allowed!

Cell# M23: Black Cloud — Meta 3: Can transform into gaseous clouds emitting toxic fumes. Danger: do not enter under any circumstance! Do not break door seal!

Cell# M25: Berserker — Meta 3: Can transform into a giant beast of inhuman strength. Danger: do not enter under any circumstance! Beware of pet dander!

When we reach cell M27 all the hairs on my neck

stand on end.

Cell #M27: Meta-Taker — Meta 3: Can duplicate the powers of any Meta. Danger: do not enter under any circumstance! Do not leave unmonitored!

I'm instantly transported back to my face-to-face encounter with Meta-Taker. I can see his chalky white skin. Smell his hot, rotten breath.

I can't believe it. The Worm did it! He actually freed the most dangerous Metas on the planet. And then I realize, we're only in the Meta-morph wing. What about all the Meta 3 Psychics? Or the Meta 3 Energy Manipulators? Or ...

I grab K'ami's arm. "We can't win this! We've got to get out of here!"

K'ami slaps me hard across the face. Boy, does she love doing that.

"Elliott Harkness," she says. "You are the savior of the universe and your planet's only hope. Pull yourself together."

I feel ashamed. She's right. I have to pull myself together. My whole life I've been dreaming of being a Meta. Now, without my family here, it's all up to me. I can't let them down. Even if I die, I'm going to make them proud. I start running her words through my mind over and over again. *Never show weakness. Never show weakness. Never show weakness.*

K'ami points to the end of the hallway at yet another set of double doors. "The Orb of Oblivion is through there."

We approach slowly. Both of us know that whatever's standing behind these doors may be the last thing we ever see.

I look at K'ami and she nods. I take a deep breath.

Never show weakness.

Then I push the doors open.

FROM THE META MONITOR:

Meta Profile

Name: Dog-Gone
Role: Hero   Status: Active

VITALS:

Breed: German Shepherd
Real Name: Dog-Gone
Height: 2'1" (at shoulder)
Weight: 85 lbs
Eye Color: Dark Brown
Hair Color: Brown/Black

META POWERS:

Class: Meta-morph
Power Level: ██ ██
- **Considerable Invisibility**
- **Can turn all or part of body invisible**

CHARACTERISTICS:

Combat	45	████
Durability	16	█
Leadership	10	█
Strategy	12	█
Willpower	56	████

THIRTEEN

I BATTLE A SLIMY WORM TO THE DEATH

"Come on out," The Worm squeals. "Welcome to your funeral."

The doors let out to a massive courtyard that's roughly the size of two football fields, and open to the night sky. It has an uneven octagonal shape formed by the walls of the eight building wings. Fittingly, it feels like we're stepping into the Roman Colosseum.

The Worm stands proudly in the center, surrounded by the greatest army of Meta 3 villains ever assembled.

"Oh, man," I whisper to K'ami. "This is exactly what I was afraid of. They're all here."

"Who are they?" she whispers back.

"Only the most dangerous supervillains on the

planet," I whisper. "Strongmen, Speedsters, Psychics, Magicians, Flyers, Energy Manipulators, Intellects, and last, but not least, the Meta-morphs. There must be over fifty of them."

With all of their various sizes, shapes, and colors, it's like staring into a kaleidoscope of terror. I quickly pinpoint Meta-Taker, who is standing to the Worm's left.

My whole body is trembling. Beads of sweat trickle down my temples. I take a deep breath and then K'ami and I enter the arena, stopping twenty yards from the Worm.

I scan the villains. "Look at their faces, they're all blank. The Worm and the Orb are controlling them."

Out of the corner of my eye, I catch a flash of movement in the back of the motionless crowd. It's Makeshift. He's rocking back and forth like he's nervous.

Before we left the Meta-morph wing, I stuffed the Sheeld into my front pants pocket. It's bulging slightly so I try to cover it with my hand as naturally as possible.

This is really it. The final showdown. I have no clue how this is going to go down. I don't know if we should try to negotiate or just attack.

But apparently, K'ami has her own ideas.

"The power of the Orb is wasted on you," she says, and spits in the Worm's general direction.

The Worm sneers. "Oh, I've been waiting for you, K'ami Sollarr," he says, gripping the Orb of Oblivion. "It appears we have a lot in common, don't we? Probably more than you care to admit. Tell me, did you clue in your little friend about our conversations?"

"What?" I say, turning to K'ami. "What conversations?"

"Do not listen to him," she says. But she won't look at me.

"I see you have not," says the Worm. "Well, your partner and I have become quite close over the past few days. Both of us trying to use the Orb to overpower one another. But as they say on our world, possession is nine-tenths of the law. My claim is much, much stronger. However, our little mind chats helped me learn that you had defeated the morons I sent to the Waystation. I'd given them the simple task of retrieving the blueprints so I could free my friends here, but I never really expected them to succeed. Turns out, I didn't need them anyway." Then he looks directly at K'ami, "Thanks to you."

"Be silent," K'ami whispers.

"Don't you think the boy deserves to know the truth?" asks the Worm.

"What's he talking about?" I demand. "What's going on?"

"What's going on," says the Worm, "is that your friend here told me how to free this guy." The Worm puts his hand on Meta-Taker's shoulder. "Once she gave me all the details about his cell, I was able to take him out of suspended animation. All I needed to do was get in through the air vent. It took me about fifteen minutes. Of course, it took him a little longer to regain consciousness. And boy was he peeved when he woke up! But all I needed," he says petting the Orb, "was a little mind control magic to get him back in line."

"You told him about Meta-Taker's cell?" I yell at K'ami.

"No!" she says defiantly. "He controlled me. He made me ask you, and then he stole it from my mind."

"And once I had Meta-Taker," The Worm continues, "he was like a Swiss Army Knife to help free the Intellects. Then I used *their* brainpower to bust out the rest."

My mind races back to everything K'ami and I have gone through. What other secrets did she reveal? My weird powers? The Sheeld? I feel more confused than ever. Can I still trust her? Now I don't know what to do.

"You do not understand the scope of the power you possess," K'ami says. "The Orb will destroy you."

"Oh, trust me," The Worm laughs. "There's nothing overly complex here. It's quite simple actually. You see, whatever I want, I get. Like your death for instance."

The Worm clutches the Orb with both hands.

"Wait!" I yell, stepping in front of K'ami. "If you're going to kill her, first you've got to go through me."

"Elliott, no!" K'ami orders.

"Is this a joke?" The Worm says, laughing aloud. "So, what are you saying?"

"I'm saying that I challenge you to a battle to the

death. You think you were ignored? You think you were nothing? Imagine growing up powerless in a family of superheroes. Do you think anyone really pays attention to you? Do you think anyone really cares what your grades are, or if you have friends, or ... if it's your freaking birthday?"

The Worm just stares at me.

"Well, I can tell you they don't. They tell you you're part of the family—part of the team. But you know in your heart of hearts that they're just humoring you—that they're trying not to hurt your feelings, because your pitiful life isn't where all the glory is. So, I know *exactly* how you feel. And, you know what? I'm tired of it. That's not how I'm going to go down!"

"Fine," says the Worm. "Do you want me to kill you with Black Cloud or someone else?"

"No," I say. "I want *you* to do it. You may be the master of a Meta 3 army, but behind those blank stares, I bet none of them have an ounce of respect for you. I mean, who can respect a Meta 1 that can't even kill a twelve-year-old Zero?"

The Worm turns to his army. They stand motionless, but then Makeshift leans out and shrugs his shoulders.

"Very well," the Worm says. "As you wish. Makeshift, keep an eye on the girl."

"No Orb," I say. "You do it on your own."

"I won't need the Orb, boy" he says, confidently.

We square off. I quickly recall everything I can about

his Meta profile. Based on his fighting tendencies, his favorite move is to burrow underground and re-emerge behind his victim for a sneak attack. And then, he'll do it again and again until he wins. I feel pretty confident I've got his number.

His problem is that he doesn't have mine.

I crouch into the low frontal karate stance Shadow Hawk taught me, maintaining my balance to easily shift from defense to offense without losing energy.

I wait for him to strike first.

"What are you standing around for?" I say. "Are you afraid of me?"

"Hardly," he sneers.

Then, as expected, he dives to go underground. Unfortunately, his head smashes hard on the surface and his body topples over.

"Take that!" I say, and deliver a blow to his solar plexus. Then, just as Shadow Hawk taught me, I get out.

The Worm scrambles to his feet, shaken and wheezing. "Lucky," he says. "Must be special soil here." His face is bright red. He turns to see if his army is still watching. They are. "Now you've made me angry!" This time he tries the same move, but to his left. He slams into the ground again and flips onto his back. I move in and kick him in the ribs.

He coughs violently and pulls himself up to one knee. He's dizzy. Disoriented. He staggers to his feet. "My powers? What are you doing to me?"

"Oh," I say, "I'm simply doing the same thing to your powers that you did to my family." Then I sock him square in the jaw. "I'm getting rid of them!" The Worm falls backwards and several of his teeth go flying.

I bend over in pain. My hand is on fire. It feels like it's broken.

"Elliott!" K'ami yells.

I spin to find the Worm lying flat on his back, both of his hands on the Orb.

"You tricked me! But now your little game is over," says the Worm, holding the Orb up over his head.

Suddenly, my head starts throbbing. It feels like my brain is being squeezed to a pulp. I hear his voice trying to enter my mind.

I try to resist it, to push it back out, but the force is overwhelming. One thought starts to build up inside of me—one word that will release all of the pressure. I build it up and build it up. And then, I release it like a raging volcano.

OUT!

The Worm screams. It's a terrible, high-pitched scream. Then his eyes go white, and he flops over like a limp noodle.

I look over at K'ami. She's also holding her head. Somehow, probably through her psychic link with the Orb, my thoughts impacted her also.

"W-What did you do to him?" Makeshift asks.

"Stay back!" I warn. "Or, I'll do the same to you!"

Then I look at the Worm's body. K'ami is huddled over him.

"K'ami, wait! What are you doing? I have the Sheeld."

"I'm sorry, Elliott," she says. And then she turns towards me, the Orb of Oblivion in her bare hands.

"KABOOM!" came a thundering pop from above, and I cover my ears to dull the sound. And then it gets dark, like some giant planet is blocking the moonlight.

I look up and see an enormous spaceship hovering above us.

The Blood Bringers have arrived.

FROM THE META MONITOR:

Meta Profile

Name: Makeshift
Role: Villain   Status: Active

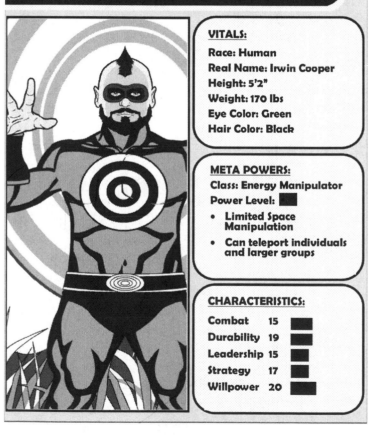

VITALS:

Race: Human
Real Name: Irwin Cooper
Height: 5'2"
Weight: 170 lbs
Eye Color: Green
Hair Color: Black

META POWERS:

Class: Energy Manipulator
Power Level:

- Limited Space Manipulation
- Can teleport individuals and larger groups

CHARACTERISTICS:

Combat	15	
Durability	19	
Leadership	15	
Strategy	17	
Willpower	20	

FOURTEEN

I TAKE CONTROL OF ABSOLUTELY EVERYTHING

So much is happening it's impossible to keep track. K'ami is holding the Orb of Oblivion, a spaceship chock-full of blood-thirsty aliens is floating over our heads, the Worm is an unconscious vegetable, and all the Meta 3 villains are slowly regaining their wits.

And, oh yeah, apparently I'm the only sane person in the entire zip code.

I don't even know where to begin.

"W-What is that thing?" Makeshift asks, looking up.

"Oh, that?" I say. "That's some really, really bad news."

It's time to focus. The one thing all this craziness has in common is the Orb. I have to get it out of K'ami's hands and safely into the Sheeld. Then we've got to get out of here, before the Blood Brigade get their paws on it. I pull out the Sheeld and rub its underside. It opens up like a Hungry Hungry Hippo.

"Quick, K'ami!" I yell. Drop the Orb into the clammy thing!"

But she doesn't respond. It's like she's frozen in a block of ice. Her eyes are closed. Her head tilted towards the sky. "Such power," she mutters in a kind of daze. "I never imagined such power."

"K'ami! Can you hear me? Let! Go! Of! The! Orb!"

She turns and opens her eyes. Her pupils are dancing like flames. "No, Elliott Harkness," she says. "This is our only chance."

"Our only chance?" I say. "For what?"

"For survival," she says. "That is a Blood Bringer warship. No one ever escapes the Blood Bringers alive."

Just then, all sorts of noises erupt from high above. I look up to see a giant hole opening in the side of the warship. The next thing I know, dozens of smaller ships come pouring out and start flying towards us. There's no time to lose. Things are about to go freaking nuts.

"K'ami!" I order. "Put the Orb in the Sheeld!"

But it's too late. Within seconds, the smaller ships hit the ground, dumping waves of Blood Bringer soldiers into the courtyard. The aliens form a giant circle around us, including the Meta villains, many of whom have now fully recovered from the Worm's mind control and are completely confused by what's happening.

I take in our new situation. As far as my limited knowledge of alien warrior species goes, The Blood Bringers are an impressive group. Each of them is Sumo-sized and covered head-to-toe in some sort of leathery brown armor, the texture of which seems strangely familiar. They are carrying long, spear-like weapons with huge blades fixed to the ends. It seems like there's hundreds of them. I try to take a quick count, but can't keep up. And it doesn't really matter anyway. We're totally outnumbered.

Makeshift drops into the fetal position and starts whimpering.

Suddenly, a group of Blood Bringers part and the biggest, baddest one I've seen yet steps forward. He's also outfitted in head-to-toe armor, but wears a long, gold cape and carries the largest weapon of the bunch. He stops about thirty yards from us, his piercing green eyes scanning us from beneath his helmet. Could this be the Emperor?

"Welcome to Earth, G'rarr Mongrell, High Commander of the Blood Brigade," K'ami says with a respectful nod. "I see our esteemed Emperor did not wish to get his hands dirty."

"K'ami Sollarr," the High Commander says, "Does your insolence know no bounds? Traitors are not permitted to use the name of the Emperor, the Lord of the Universe, in vain. Besides, you know all too well that killing is the birthright of the Blood Brigade."

"I do know this," she says. "Just as you know that I am in possession of the Orb of Oblivion, the very object I am certain you are here to retrieve. Fortunately, I am feeling generous. I will give you one chance to call off your hounds and I shall consider sparing your life. If you choose otherwise, I regret to inform you that you, and all of your beasts, will die a painful, honorless death."

The High Commander delivers a deep, hearty laugh that rattles my bones. "Little girl," he says. "Do you forget to whom you are speaking? I am the High Commander of the Blood Bringers. I am the Destroyer of Worlds. I am the Harbinger of Death. Hand over the Orb immediately and I promise your ending will be a swift one. I cannot, however, promise the same for your lowly, earth-dwelling allies."

I hear growling and other bodily noises behind me. The Meta villains are getting restless.

But K'ami doesn't move. Instead she gives a wry smile. "I know exactly to whom I speak, High Commander. Your offer is quite fair, but I fear you have chosen unwisely. Prepare to die."

The Orb begins to pulsate.

But nothing happens.

K'ami looks at the Orb, and then back to the High Commander. But he's just standing there, watching her. What's going on? Why didn't the Orb do its thing?

Then the giant takes a step forward. "Foolish girl," he

says. "Did you not think that we would prepare properly for a battle with the Orb of Oblivion? Your father was a traitor, but his research for the Emperor was quite thorough. That is why our armor is made entirely from Sheelds."

K'ami gives a look of surprise.

And before I can move, the High Commander points his weapon and fires a laser blast right through her.

K'ami falls backwards.

I catch her before she hits the ground.

"Kill them!" the High Commander orders. "Kill them all!"

Suddenly, there's a loud roar and a white blur appears, delivering a powerful right hook to the High Commander's face. It's Meta-Taker!

There is a moment of stunned silence. And then a massive brawl erupts between the Meta villains and Blood Bringers.

I cradle K'ami in my arms. She's been shot clean through the chest. She's struggling to breathe, her whole body is shaking. Blackish blood is flowing everywhere.

"K'ami," I plead. "K'ami? Can you hear me?"

"E-Elliott," she says, coughing several times. "I-I am sorry. I-I thought with the Orb I could ... save us. B-but I failed."

Tears stream down my cheeks. "K'ami, hang on. You're not going to die. You can't die."

She smiles feebly and squeezes my hand. "No, it is too

late ... for me."

"No, we'll find a way out of this," I cry. "I promise. We always do."

"No, Elliot," she says. "P-Please, take the Orb in the Sheeld and finish what my father started. You will always be my good friend. M-My ... B ... FF ... N-Never ... show ... weak ... "

And then, her green eyes roll back in her head.

She's gone.

I sit for a moment, holding her lifeless body in my arms.

And then, I yell.

I yell with grief.

I yell in anger.

I look up. A massive battle rages around us, but everything seems like it's moving in slow motion. The fighting has mushroomed from the courtyard to inside the buildings and even up to the sky. The Meta 3 villains are fighting for their lives. I spot the High Commander who is now mired in combat with Meta-Taker and several other villains at once.

It feels like I'm in a strange dream. A dream I can't escape from. And then, I hear someone calling me. It's faint at first, then it grows stronger and stronger.

Has everyone else forgotten about it?

It's the one behind all of this death. All of this destruction. I look down at K'ami's body and there it sits, resting innocently in her hands.

The Orb of Oblivion.

I know I should put it in the Sheeld. Just lock it in the Sheeld and make a run for it. Run to safety, and then figure out what to do next.

But, I'm tired of running.

I'm tired of playing it safe. I'm tired of being a victim.

I want to take control.

I know what I need to do.

I reach down and grab the Orb.

And everything shifts.

I feel a sudden, immense surge of power flowing through me. My body feels electric. I feel lighter. Like every molecule of my being is floating on air. It feels like I can do anything.

"And now you can," says a strange voice. *"Now you can be the greatest Meta that every walked the planet. Isn't that what you always wanted?"*

Where is that voice coming from? It sounds so familiar. It sounds like ... me?

"That's because it is you, Elliott," it says. *"You have always had the power inside of you. You just never knew how to access it."*

"Who are you?" I say.

"I'm you," it says. *"I'm a better version of you. I'm the person you have always wanted to be. Popular. Powerful. Proud. And now, you can have everything you've always wanted. Now it's all within your reach. Fame. Friends. Fans."*

"No," I say. "You're not me. I know who you are. I know what you are."

"*Elliott,*" it says quickly. "*Don't be hasty. I understand it may take a while for you to adjust to your newfound powers. But if you'll just trust—*"

"No," I say. "I won't let you leech off me. I'm going to be in control."

"*Elliott,*" it says, its voice sounding more desperate. "*Just give me a chance. Give us a—*"

"I! SAID! NO!"

I push back with all of my will. I push back with all of my soul. I push back like my life depends on it.

And then, I feel the Orb flinch. Bend. Scream.

I surround it with my will. I overpower it.

I feel it succumb to my will.

And then, I master it.

The Orb of Oblivion is now under my control.

I open my eyes.

The battle is still going strong. It's clear the Blood Bringers are well trained and far more organized than I imagined. They've pressed the Meta villains into a corner. The Metas are fighting individual battles. The Metas are losing.

I realize what I need to do. Then I feel a tap on my shoulder. Makeshift is standing behind me. I make a fist.

"Wait!" Makeshift says quickly. "I think I can help you. See, your family isn't really dead."

"What?" I say. "What are you talking about?"

"Well," the little man continues, "See, my powers are kind of strange. I call myself Makeshift because I can 'make' things 'shift.' Get it? You know, like teleport. So things don't die when I send them away. I only shift them into a pocket dimension. I call it 'Exile.' It's an alternate universe that's like Earth, but it's not. Anyway, I can try to bring them back. If you want me to?"

I grab him by the shoulders. "Yes!" I say. "Yes! Do it now!"

"Well, okay," says Makeshift. Then I watch as he stretches out his hands, and a familiar yellow circle appears. It expands like a giant rubber band, moving faster and faster, and then, with a loud WHOOSH, it disappears. In its place, stands seven surprised figures.

My family!

They're all there: Mom, Dad, Grace, Shadow Hawk, Master Mime, Blue Bolt and TechnocRat. The Freedom Force is back!

I run into my parent's arms.

"Elliott," Mom says. "Where have you been?"

But I'm so overwhelmed, I can't answer. It feels so great to have them back.

"Um, forget about him," says Grace. "What the heck's going on out there?"

They turn towards the war, and their eyes pop out of their sockets.

"Holy guacamole," TechnocRat whispers.

"There's no time for details," I say. "We need to help

the bad guys beat the aliens. All of you know how to lead a team into battle. Mom, you take the Psychics. Dad, you've got the Strongmen. Grace, take the Flyers. Shadow Hawk, the Energy Manipulators. TechnocRat's got the Intellects, Master Mime the Magicians, and Blue Bolt the Speedsters. I'll take the Meta-morphs. Now let's go!"

I start into the fray, but the Freedom Force is glued to their spots.

"I said, let's go!"

"But, Elliott," Dad says, "these guys are dangerous. What makes you think they'll listen to us?"

"You're right," I say, flashing the Orb. "They won't listen to you. But I know they'll listen to me."

I focus on the Orb and it starts to pulsate. I use the Orb's power to access my knowledge of each and every Meta profile and then push this knowledge out, planting this information into the minds of each villain. Then, I command them to stop fighting independently, and to reorganize into their respective Meta power classifications. Suddenly, the villains start to re-form, fighting no longer as individuals, but as teams.

"There, now they're ready for you." I turn to the Freedom Force, but they're just standing there with their jaws hanging open.

"Oh, and see that big one over there?" I say, pointing to the High Commander.

They nod.

"That one's mine. Got it?"

They nod again.

"Okay then," I say. "Let's go!"

"Well, you heard the man," Dad says. "Freedom Force—it's Fight Time!"

I lead the way, and they follow *me* into battle.

FROM THE META MONITOR:

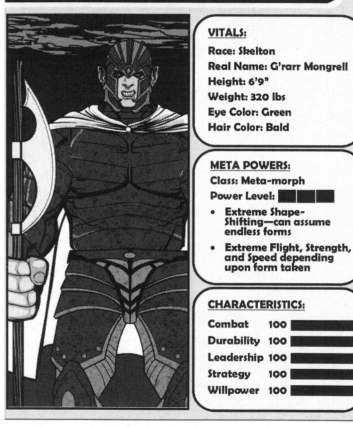

Meta Profile

Name: High Commander
Role: Villain   Status: Active

VITALS:

Race: Skelton
Real Name: G'rarr Mongrell
Height: 6'9"
Weight: 320 lbs
Eye Color: Green
Hair Color: Bald

META POWERS:

Class: Meta-morph
Power Level: ▮▮▮

- Extreme Shape-Shifting—can assume endless forms
- Extreme Flight, Strength, and Speed depending upon form taken

CHARACTERISTICS:

Combat	100	
Durability	100	
Leadership	100	
Strategy	100	
Willpower	100	

FIFTEEN

I DOOM THE ENTIRE FREAKING UNIVERSE

With the Freedom Force's leadership, the tide turns quickly.

Dad and Blue Bolt join the Strongmen and Speedsters together and strike at the heart of the Blood Brigade army. Mom and Shadow Hawk spread out the Psychics and Energy Manipulators and start picking off victims one by one. Grace takes her Flyers airborne to stop the flow of incoming spaceships, while Master Mime and his Magicians provide ground cover. TechnocRat collects his Intellects and disappears inside the prison for reasons I can't begin to fathom.

But, I don't have time to sit around gawking.

I have to save the world.

My Meta-morphs are fighting on the far side of the courtyard, and I'm struggling to make my way over without getting dismembered, or worse, losing hold of all the Meta villains under my control. I dodge the metal leg of Retractable Man, vault over Tumbler, and use Ripcord as a slingshot. After avoiding a barrage of crossfire, I finally make it.

The Meta-morphs are more than holding their own. Flameout has a group of Blood Bringers pinned behind a giant wall of fire. Black Cloud is storming over packs of victims. The Berserker is doing his best impression of King Kong, swatting any ships that manage to break through the blockade that Grace and the Flyers have setup. But, the Meta-morph I need is engaged in an epic battle with the High Commander.

Meta-Taker.

To my surprise, the High Commander is matching him blow for blow. Clearly, the High Commander is no ordinary Skelton. And if he can hang with a powerhouse like Meta-Taker, then just how strong is this guy?

I decide to find out.

I tap into the Orb and send a command into Meta-Taker's brain. *Power up! Power up until you can't power up anymore!*

Meta-Taker stops, and then stretches out his arms. I feel a strange sensation radiating from his mind. Then the orange energy from his eyes spills out in every direction. It's as if his whole being is unlocking—like every cell in his body is opening up, drawing in all of the Meta powers around him. Through his mind, I can feel the energy building up in his veins. It feels incredible. It feels like he's on a completely different level.

It feels like he's at Meta 4.

Now let's see what this bad boy can do.

I send the command to attack and Meta-Taker charges the High Commander at ridiculous speed, plowing the alien into the building behind him with such force the entire structure collapses on top of them. Then Meta-Taker emerges from the rubble and bombards the High Commander with a flurry of pulsar beams, concussion blasts, and lightning strikes, resulting in a gigantic explosion that sends debris flying everywhere.

I order Meta-Taker to pull back. The air is so thick with smoke it's impossible to see anything. For any normal foe, that probably would be the end of the story, but I know the High Commander isn't any normal foe.

That's when I feel the ground trembling beneath my feet. And then, as the smoke starts to clear, I see humungous chunks of concrete being tossed aside like throw pillows. The next thing I know, something very large shoots up into the air and lands with a earth-shattering thud. But, that "something" isn't the High Commander at all.

The creature stands over two stories tall. At first, it appears almost ape-like, but with deep, red eyes and matted green fur covering every inch of its immense, muscled body. It pounds its chest and lets out a deafening roar from between razor-sharp teeth. And then, out of nowhere, it unfolds a giant pair of bat-like wings and makes an unbelievable fifty-foot leap straight into the chest of Meta-Taker. Meta-Taker crashes through a wall.

Now I can see why the Blood Bringers are an unstoppable killing force. And from what K'ami told me, I'm guessing this is just one of the horrific forms the High Commander can adopt. Even at Meta 4, I can't imagine how Meta-Taker will possibly win this fight.

But Meta-Taker brushes himself off, and squares up to his enemy. Then the villain activates his orange flames again, reaching out to draw in even more Meta power. What is he doing? Is he trying to reach Meta 5?

The creature doesn't wait to find out. Instead, it extends its giant wings and takes to the air again.

Before Meta-Taker can strike, his body starts to swell, his muscles inflating to grotesque proportions. It looks like he may have drawn in too much power. More power than he can possibly contain.

I frantically try to reverse my instructions. *Power down! Power down!* But, it's too late. Meta-Taker is frozen in place. He looks like a giant balloon.

Then, the creature drops in front of Meta-Taker, opens its jaws and snaps down.

The explosion is massive.

I'm instantly blown off my feet. All I can think about is holding on to the Orb. My body smashes into something hard and unforgiving, knocking the wind out of me.

I find myself lying on the ground, covered in rubble. I'm still alive, except, in addition to a broken hand, I now have incredibly sore ribs. I draw the Orb close to my chest. Somehow, I managed to hang on to it.

The explosion was so blinding it takes a few seconds for my eyes to readjust. But when they do, I can't believe what I'm seeing. Everything within a twenty-yard radius of Meta-Taker has been completely vaporized. Flameout. Black Cloud. The Berserker. Everything and everyone is gone. Except for—

"No more games, earthling," says The High Commander, "Give me the Orb and I will let the girl live." The High Commander stands no more than ten feet away. Somehow he survived the blast and is now back to his original form. I notice immediately that most of his armor is shredded. And, more importantly, he's missing his helmet. He must have ditched it when he turned into that monster. That means I can use the Orb on him! But then I realize what he said, and who he's holding.

Grace is hanging face-up beneath one of his massive arms. His other hand is wrapped firmly around her neck. Meta-Taker's blast must have been so powerful that it knocked Grace right out of the sky. And the High Commander is gripping her so tightly she's struggling to breathe. The terror in her eyes says all I need to know. I can't risk using the Orb on him when simply closing his hand would instantly crush her throat.

But, I can't just turn over the Orb either.

"If I give you the Orb, you'll kill us all," I say.

"Perhaps," he says. "But, I was not sent to your world to destroy it. My mission was to achieve two objectives. I have accomplished the first, and I will not leave until I complete the second."

My blood starts boiling. "So I take it murdering a girl was one of your objectives."

"K'ami Sollarr was a traitor," he says. "She killed five guards during her escape. She was a dangerous criminal."

"She was my friend!" I shout. "My best friend! Better than you, or your stinking Emperor or your whole freaking planet!"

He smiles. It's strange to see his face so clearly. He looks just like K'ami's father, but with a squarer jaw and a large diagonal scar that runs from his forehead, across his left eye and down his cheek. "My hand is getting tired," he says. "So, I suggest we discuss my original bargain. Give me the Orb and I will give you the girl."

By now, I realize that all the fighting has stopped. Everyone is watching us, waiting for my response. The fate of the whole universe is hanging on my word.

Out of the corner of my eye, I catch the worried looks of my parents. I need more time to think, but I don't have it. I need to stall.

"What assurances will you offer me?" I ask.

"I offer you my word," The High Commander says.

"On my world, our word is our currency. I give you my word that if you give me the Orb of Oblivion, I will leave you in peace."

If I've learned anything in this mess it's two things. One, my track record trusting Skeltons is not a good one. Two, if I don't give him the Orb then Grace is a goner. I don't have time to think this through. But then, I realize I'm not alone in this either.

I reach out in my mind.

"Orb?" I say. *"Who is your one true master?"*

"You, Elliott Harkness," the Orb answers. *"You are my one true master."*

"I'm glad to hear that," I say. *"Once, a very good friend told me a story about how you convinced a star to explode. Was that story true?"*

"Yes," says the Orb. *"I was weak—waning and insignificant. I convinced the star to give up its life for me so that I could become significant again."*

"Yes," I say. *"And you did become significant again. Very significant. That was selfless of the star, wasn't it? Sacrificing its life for such a great cause."*

"Yes," says the Orb. *"Yes, it was."*

"What have you decided, earthling?" The High Commander demands.

I look at Grace's terrified face. "Order your men back to your warship. All of them. Now."

"Very well," the High Commander says, raising an

eyebrow. "Pull back! All of you!"

We watch as the Blood Bringers follow his orders, filing back into their spaceships and heading up to the larger warship in the sky. Only the High Commander and one ship remain.

"Well?" The High Commander asks. "Will you complete the bargain and grant me safe passage to my ship?"

"First," I say, "release the girl."

The High Commander laughs. "Do you take me for a fool? As soon as I give you the girl you will attack me with the Orb. Instead we will do the exchange simultaneously. And then, you will allow me to go back to my ship unharmed. Agreed?"

I hesitate for a moment. What choice do I have?

"I'll give you safe passage to your ship. When you reach your ship, you'll turn around immediately and head back to your planet. You'll leave mine unharmed. Deal?"

"Agreed," he says.

"On the count of three then. One ... two ... three ... "

He throws Grace to me, and I flip him the Orb.

Grace crumples in my arms. "Thank you," she says crying. "Thank you, Elliott."

The High Commander catches the Orb in his bare hands. "The Orb of Oblivion," he whispers.

"Now, go!" I command. "And never return!"

The High Commander looks up like he's startled. Like he forgot I'm even here. "Yes, I gave you my word."

"As did I," I respond. I throw him the Sheeld Box.

He catches it and hesitates before putting the Orb inside. Then he snaps it shut.

The High Commander nods and then returns to his spaceship. We watch it lift off and then reconnect with the warship above.

Makeshift peers around a corner, "Um, did you just doom all of humanity?"

"Possibly," I say. "But I don't think so."

Just then, TechnocRat comes scampering out of Lockdown. "Elliott, the Intellects and I fixed all the Meta 3 cells. I thought I should put all that brain power to good use. Now we need to get these villains locked up again. I already secured my bunch."

So that's where he went! Man, I love that rat.

I look up at the sky. The warship starts turning away from Earth. I still don't trust that some giant laser beam isn't going to come firing down on us, blasting us all to smithereens.

"Dad," I say. "Can you and the Freedom Force make sure you get all these villains back in their cells? And I suggest you do it as quickly as possible."

"Sure, Elliott," Dad says. "Team, let's move!" Then he stops and looks at Makeshift. "What about this guy?"

"He's okay. Leave him with me."

Makeshift and I stand for a while, watching the warship maneuver.

"Wait a minute," Makeshift says. "Are you still

controlling the Meta 3's?"

"Yep," I say.

"But you're not holding the Orb," Makeshift says.

"Nope. I realized I didn't have to."

Just then, the ship kicks on its jets and enters hyper-speed, disappearing into the night sky. The High Commander kept his word. And so had I.

I close my eyes and reach out to the orb. I can still feel our connection.

"Orb," I say. *"It's time."*

"Yes," the Orb says. *"I am ready."*

"Thank you," I say. *"You will shine as the brightest star in the universe for all eternity."*

"Never show weakness," says the Orb.

"Yes," I say. *"Never show weakness."*

And then, somewhere in the distant galaxy, the Orb of Oblivion sacrifices its life and a Blood Brigade warship explodes into a brilliant flash of nothingness.

FROM THE META MONITOR:

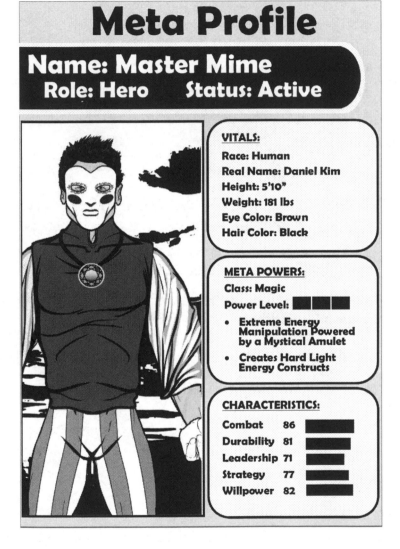

Meta Profile

Name: Master Mime
Role: Hero   **Status: Active**

VITALS:

Race: Human
Real Name: Daniel Kim
Height: 5'10"
Weight: 181 lbs
Eye Color: Brown
Hair Color: Black

META POWERS:

Class: Magic
Power Level: ■ ■ ■

- **Extreme Energy Manipulation Powered by a Mystical Amulet**
- **Creates Hard Light Energy Constructs**

CHARACTERISTICS:

Combat	86	■■■
Durability	81	■■■
Leadership	71	■■■
Strategy	77	■■■
Willpower	82	■■■

EPILOGUE

THREE VERY LONG MONTHS LATER...

I hop into the command chair and set the Meta Monitor on manual control. It's Friday night, the busiest night of the week, and I'm hoping to get lucky. It's been months since I could use my right hand, but now that my cast is off, I'm itching for some action.

I brought popcorn with me, so I set the cameras to cycle through The Waystation to spot any furry predators. Not that I can find Dog-Gone anyway—especially if he's in stealth mode. Note to self: get TechnocRat to install heat-seeking cameras.

My Dad is in the lab, analyzing my powers. Ever since Lockdown, he and TechnocRat have run me through a whole battery of tests. Apparently, my powers are similar to only one other Meta they've seen before. Meta-Taker. They realized in testing me that perhaps they misclassified him. Our powers are so unique, they don't fit within any of the eight standard Meta classifications. So, they created a new one.

They're calling it Meta Manipulation.

We're still trying to make sense of it, but while Meta-Taker could absorb and use the powers of others, I can manipulate, and even nullify, the Meta powers of others. I found this surprising at first, but then, I thought back to all the stuff that's happened to me. Like when the Worm tried to kill me, but couldn't use his powers. Or when Taser tried to fry me, but his electricity bounced off my chest. Or, how I cancelled Meta-Taker's powers when he tried to take mine.

Or, how I was the only one that could control the Orb of Oblivion.

The strange thing is that my powers seem to be reactive in nature. So, they could have been there all along. I was just never in a dangerous enough situation with Metas to bring them out. Which also made me wonder if Mom could really read my mind in the first place?

It's funny how life can kick you in the teeth.

I keep cycling through the Waystation cameras.

Speaking of Mom, I find her in the Bulk Transporter Room, unloading boxes from the Prop House. We decided to put the Prop House up for sale. After those

Meta 1 morons broke in, we just didn't feel safe using it anymore. I mean, who knows how many of their friends they talked to? So, we packed everything up. Of course, we removed the Transporter and all signs of our Meta existence. In the meantime, Grace and I are being homeschooled by the Freedom Force. Shadow Hawk is my favorite teacher, he likes to ditch the books and take us to the Combat Room for a real education.

And, not surprisingly, it's in the Combat Room where I find him. He and Blue Bolt are working on a few new moves together. It looks like they pulled up a robot assault scenario and are competing on who can disable them faster. I know Blue Bolt's a Meta 3 Speedster, but I'd never bet against Shadow Hawk.

TechnocRat and Master Mime are in the Hangar. TechnocRat refuses to let Master Mime pilot anything until he completes at least 1,000 hours in the flight simulator. I can't blame him. He's just spent months building the Freedom Flyer III. He keeps saying this one is the best version ever. And he's right, because it's made with Skelton technology.

After Lockdown, we took K'ami's body to the site of her father's crash-landing. I thought it's only fitting that they be buried together. The Freedom Force helped to clear the area and we gave her a hero's funeral. I think about her a lot. She made me realize it's important to stand up for what you believe in. And, the most important thing is to always believe in yourself.

It's strange, but I keep expecting to hear something from the Emperor. Sometimes I find myself waking up in the middle of the night drenched in sweat. I know I've had a nightmare, but I can't seem to remember what it was about. Mom says not to worry. It's probably just my mind processing everything that's happened. Maybe she's right, but I get a weird feeling every time it happens.

Speaking of weird, let's talk about Grace. Ever since Lockdown, it's like she's had a brain transplant. Suddenly, she's my new best friend. We started hanging out, doing stuff and laughing together. Now don't get me wrong, we still have our moments, but they're much less frequent. I tease her all the time about saving her life, but I also tell her I'm glad she's my big sister.

I finally find Dog-Gone in the Galley. It looks like my popcorn is safe because he's splitting an ice cream sundae with Makeshift. We realized Makeshift wasn't such a bad guy after all. He'd just gotten mixed up with the wrong crowd. So we sort of adopted him. He's not a full-fledged member of the Freedom Force yet, but he's proving himself every day. It looks like his next challenge will be cleaning up the mess I'm sure Dog-Gone is going to deliver.

Yep, it's just another day on the Waystation.

If only something would happen.

"Meta 2 disturbance," blares the Meta Monitor. "Power signature identified as Dark Mauler. Alert! Alert! Alert!"

Yes! I'm finally going to see some action!

I leap out of my chair and sail down the stairs to the Mission Room to meet the team. But, to my surprise, they're already there ...

"Elliott," Dad says smiling. "Now that your cast is off, the team has something for you."

Grace stands up and hands me a box. "Here, Bro. The rat and I made this for you."

I open it up. It's a costume. My costume!

It's a navy blue bodysuit and mask, with red gloves, boots and cape. On the front is a large, white Zero with a backslash through it. There's also a gold belt with a large "E." I can't believe it. It looks freaking awesome!

"So, kid," says Shadow Hawk. "You picked a name?"

"Yep," I say smiling. "You can call me—Epic Zero."

"Epic Zero?" Dad asks. "Why Epic Zero?"

"Well," I say. "The Zero is because I can turn other Metas into Zeros. And, the Epic is because I've been a Zero my whole life, and, well, I can't even begin to tell you how *freaking epic* it is to finally be here!"

"Epic Zero," Mom says. "I like it."

"Alright, enough yapping," says Grace. "It's time for Epic Zero here to make his debut. Show us what you've got, but remember one thing, don't block my good side."

She hugs me and everyone cheers.

Then, I go on my first mission as an official member of the Freedom Force. And from that day forward, I know that wherever there's evil, I'll be there.

Meta Profile

Name: Epic Zero
Role: Hero　　　Status: Active

VITALS:

Race: Human
Real Name: Elliott Harkness
Height: 4'8"
Weight: 89 lbs
Eye Color: Brown
Hair Color: Brown

META POWERS:

Class: Meta Manipulation
Powers Level: ■■■

- **Extreme Power Negation and Manipulation**
- **Vulnerable to non-Meta attack**

CHARACTERISTICS:

Combat	25	■
Durability	12	▪
Leadership	55	■■■
Strategy	65	■■■■
Willpower	77	■■■■■

META POWERS GLOSSARY

FROM THE META MONITOR:

There are eight known Meta power classifications. These classifications have been established to simplify Meta identification and provide a quick framework to understand a Meta's potential powers and capabilities. **Note:** Metas can possess powers in more than one classification. In addition, Metas can evolve over time in both the powers they express, as well as the effectiveness of their powers.

Due to the wide range of Meta abilities, superpowers have been further segmented into power levels. Power levels differ across Meta power classifications. In general, the following power levels have been established:

- Meta 0: Displays no Meta power.
- Meta 1: Displays limited Meta power.
- Meta 2: Displays considerable Meta power.
- Meta 3: Displays extreme Meta power.

The following is a brief overview of the eight Meta power classifications.

ENERGY MANIPULATION:

Energy Manipulation is the ability to generate, shape or act as a conduit, for various forms of energy. Energy Manipulators are able to control energy by focusing or redirecting energy towards a specific target or shaping/reshaping energy for a specific task. Energy Manipulators are often impervious to the forms of energy they are able to manipulate.

Examples of the types of energies utilized by Energy Manipulators include, but are not limited to:

- Atomic
- Chemical
- Cosmic
- Electricity
- Gravity
- Heat
- Light
- Magnetic
- Sound
- Space
- Time

Note: the fundamental difference between an Energy Manipulator and a Meta-morph with Energy Manipulation capability is that an Energy Manipulator does not change their physical, molecular state to either generate or transfer energy (see META-MORPH).

FLIGHT:
Flight is the ability to fly, glide or levitate above the Earth's surface without use of an external source (e.g. jetpack). Flight can be accomplished through a variety of methods, these include, but are not limited to:

- Reversing the forces of gravity
- Riding air currents
- Using planetary magnetic fields

- Wings

Metas exhibiting Flight can range from barely sustaining flight a few feet off the ground to reaching the far limits of outer space.

Often, Metas with Flight ability also display the complimentary ability of Super-Speed. However, it can be difficult to decipher if Super-Speed is a Meta power in its own right, or is simply a function of combining the Meta's Flight ability with the Earth's natural gravitational force.

MAGIC:

Magic is the ability to display a wide variety of Meta abilities by channeling the powers of a secondary magical or mystical source. Known secondary sources of Magic powers include, but are not limited to:

- Alien lifeforms
- Dark arts
- Demonic forces
- Departed souls
- Mystical spirits

Typically, the forces of Magic are channeled through an enchanted object. Known magical, enchanted objects include:

- Amulets
- Books
- Cloaks
- Gemstones

- Wands
- Weapons

Some Magicians have the ability to transport themselves into the mystical realm of their magical source. They may also have the ability to transport others into and out of these realms as well.

Note: the fundamental difference between a Magician and an Energy Manipulator is that a Magician typically channels their powers from a mystical source that likely requires use of an enchanted object to express these powers (see ENERGY MANIPULATOR).

META-MORPH:

Meta-morph is the ability to display a wide variety of Meta abilities by "morphing" all, or part, of one's physical form from one state into another. There are two sub-types of Meta-morphs:

- Physical
- Molecular

Physical morphing occurs when a Meta-morph transforms their physical state to express their powers. Physical Meta-morphs typically maintain their human physiology while exhibiting their powers (with the exception of Shape Shifters). Types of Physical morphing include, but are not limited to:

- Invisibility
- Malleability (elasticity/plasticity)
- Physical by-products (silk, toxins, etc...)

- Shape-shifting
- Size changes (larger or smaller)

Molecular morphing occurs when a Meta-morph transforms their molecular state from a normal physical state to a non-physical state to express their powers. Types of Molecular morphing include, but are not limited to:

- Fire
- Ice
- Rock
- Sand
- Steel
- Water

Note: Because Meta-morphs can display abilities that mimic all other Meta power classifications, it can be difficult to properly identify a Meta-morph upon first encounter. However, it is critical to carefully observe how their powers manifest, and, if it is through Physical or Molecular morphing, you can be certain you are dealing with a Meta-morph.

PSYCHIC:
Psychic is the ability to use one's mind as a weapon. There are two sub-types of Psychics:

- Telepaths
- Telekinetics

Telepathy is the ability to read and influence the thoughts of others. While Telepaths often do not appear to be physically intimidating, their power to penetrate minds can often result in more devastating damage than a physical assault.

Telekinesis is the ability to manipulate physical objects with one's mind. Telekinetics can often move objects with their mind that are much heavier than they could move physically. Many Telekinetics can also make objects move at very high speeds.

Note: Psychics are known to strike from long distance, and, in a fight it is advised to incapacitate them as quickly as possible. Psychics often become physically drained from extended use of their powers.

SUPER-INTELLIGENCE:
Super-Intelligence is the ability to display levels of intelligence above standard genius intellect. Super-Intelligence can manifest in many forms, including, but not limited to:

- Superior analytical ability
- Superior information synthesizing
- Superior learning capacity
- Superior reasoning skills

Note: Super-Intellects continuously push the envelope in the fields of technology, engineering, and weapons development. Super-Intellects are known to invent new approaches to accomplish previously impossible tasks. When dealing with a Super-Intellect, you should be mentally prepared to face challenges that have never been encountered before. In addition, Super-Intellects can come in all shapes and sizes. The most advanced Super-

Intellects have originated from non-human creatures.

SUPER-SPEED:
Super-Speed is the ability to display movement at remarkable physical speeds above standard levels of speed. Metas with Super-Speed often exhibit complimentary abilities to movement that include, but are not limited to:

- Enhanced endurance
- Phasing through solid objects
- Super-fast reflexes
- Time travel

Note: Metas with super-speed often have an equally super metabolism, burning thousands of calories per minute, and requiring them to eat many extra meals a day to maintain consistent energy levels. It has been observed that Metas exhibiting Super-Speed are quick thinkers, making it difficult to keep up with their thought process.

SUPER-STRENGTH:
Super-Strength is the ability to utilize muscles to display remarkable levels of physical strength above expected levels of strength. Metas with Super-Strength are able to lift or push objects that are well beyond the capability of an average member of their species. Metas exhibiting Super-Strength can range from lifting objects twice their weight to incalculable levels of strength allowing for the movement of planets.

Metas with Super-Speed often exhibit complimentary abilities to strength that include, but are not limited to:

- Earthquake generation through stomping
- Enhanced jumping
- Invulnerability
- Shockwave generation through clapping

Note: Metas with Super-Strength may not always possess this strength evenly. Metas with Super-Strength have been observed to demonstrate their powers in only one arm or one leg.

META PROFILE CHARACTERISTICS

FROM THE META MONITOR:

In addition to having a strong working knowledge of a Meta's powers and capabilities, it is also imperative to have an understanding of the key characteristics that form the core of their character. When facing or teaming up with Metas, understanding their key characteristics will help you gain deeper insight into their mentality and strategic potential.

What follows is a brief explanation of the five key characteristics you should become familiar with. **Note:** the data that appears in each Meta profile has been compiled from live field activity.

COMBAT:
The ability to defeat a foe in hand-to-hand combat.

DURABILITY:
The ability to withstand significant wear, pressure or damage.

LEADERSHIP:
The ability to lead a team of disparate personalities and powers to victory.

STRATEGY:
The ability to find, and successfully exploit, a foe's weakness.

WILLPOWER:
The ability to persevere, despite seemingly insurmountable odds.

GET MORE EPIC!

Don't miss any of the Epic action!

Get a **FREE** copy of
Epic Zero Extra: Tales of a Superhero Screw Up,
only at rlullman.com.

EPIC ZERO 2 IS AVAILABLE NOW!

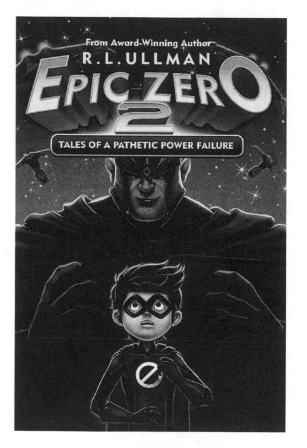

Elliott is kidnapped by a band of teenage aliens who believe he's the only one who can save the universe. But did they nab the wrong hero?

Get Epic Zero 2:
Tales of a Pathetic Power Failure today!

DO YOU HAVE MONSTER PROBLEMS?

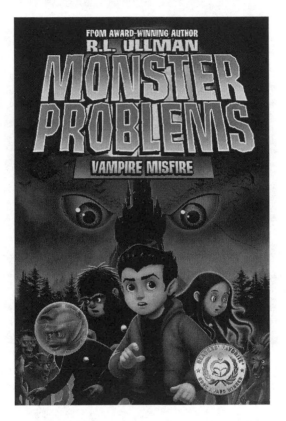

Some Monsters are Meant to be Heroes...
Readers' Favorite Book Award Winner

Life bites for a misfit kid who discovers he's the last
vampire alive and must save the world from evil monsters
in this funny, award-winning series for kids 9-12!

Get Monster Problems today!

YOU CAN MAKE A BIG DIFFERENCE

Calling all heroes! I need your help to get Epic Zero in front of more readers.

Reviews are extremely helpful in getting attention for my books. I wish I had the marketing muscle of the major publishers, but instead I have something far more valuable, loyal readers just like you! Your generosity in providing an honest review will help bring this book to the attention of more readers.

So, if you've enjoyed this book, I would be very grateful if you could spare a minute to leave a review on the book's Amazon page.

Thanks for your support!

R.L. Ullman

ABOUT THE AUTHOR

R.L. Ullman is the bestselling author of the award-winning EPIC ZERO series and the award-winning MONSTER PROBLEMS series. He creates fun, engaging page-turners that captivate the imaginations of kids and adults alike. His original, relatable characters face adventure and adversity that bring out their inner strengths. He's frequently distracted thinking up new stories, and once got lost in his own neighborhood. You can learn more about what R.L. is up to at rlullman.com, and if you see him wandering around your street please point him in the right direction home.

For news, updates, and free stuff, please sign up for the Epic Newsflash at rlullman.com.

ACKNOWLEDGMENTS

Many thanks to my team of Meta heroes for helping to bring Epic Zero to life. Thanks to my editor, Patty Walcott. Thanks to my test readers: Lauren Ullman, Jeremy Ullman, Audrey Frankel, Leslie Frankel, and Olivia Norton. Thanks to my son, Matthew, and my parents, Ken and Sandy. Finally, a mega thanks to my wife, Lynn, the stronger half of our dynamic duo for her great ideas and unwavering support.

Made in the USA
Lexington, KY
08 May 2019